Praise for *Seeking: The First Book of Journeys*

"...ideal for anyone on a quest for adventure and meaning."

—James R Coggins, Ph.D., award-winning Christian author and editor, British Columbia, Canada

"Suspense draws us into a courageous young man's escape from bondage while the allegorical nature of his story inspires us to continue our own personal journey across the Sea of Life."

— Donna Brummet, Lynch Station, Va.

"This allegorical book plants a seed of hope in a world of painful circumstances."

— Renee Rowe, LMSW, ACSW. Lake Orion, Mich.

"The book is fascinating to me because I have been at every one of those ports!"

—J. E. Arnett, Bedford, Va.

"This book portrays our common yearning to seek for the good, true and beautiful amidst life's challenges."

— Chris Long, Imlay City, Mich.

"I started reading this book late one evening and found I couldn't put it down until I had turned the last page!"

—Jan Ramsey, Lapeer, Mich.

"If you have not met Brae and the characters who interact with him in *The First Book of Journeys,* you will want to do so as soon as possible. I'm confident that your own journey will be enriched as you get to know your fellow travelers on the Sea of Life."

— Pastor Dale Hollin, Columbia Assembly of God, Mich.

"I received the book yesterday in the mail, and finished reading it tonight. Congratulations to Linda on a book well done."

— Sally Sneider, Assemblies of God Missionary

THE FIRST BOOK OF JOURNEYS

Seeking

LINDA SETTLES

EDICT HOUSE PUBLISHING, LLC
Lynchburg, Virginia

Seeking
The First Book of Journeys

For information, or to order additional copies, please contact:

Edict House Publishing Group, LLC
400 Court Street
Lynchburg, VA 24504
Phone: 434-821-4005
www.EdictHouse.com
Email: info@edicthouse.com

Cover and book design by Elizabeth Petersen, Mendocino Graphics
Book production by Cypress House
Cover and interior illustrations by Steve Ferchaud

Publisher's Cataloging-in-Publication Data:
Settles, Linda.
Seeking : the first book of journeys / Linda Settles. — 1st ed. —
Lynchburg, VA : Edict House, 2009.
p. ; cm.
(Book of journeys ; 1)
ISBN: 978-0-9790238-7-3

Summary: This allegorical work introduces us to Mercy and Grace, Regret and Sorrow in a fast paced adventure where danger and death pursue a boy who becomes a man as he seeks the Other Kingdom.
1. Other Kingdom (Imaginary place) 2. Christian fiction.
I. Title. II. Series.
PS3619.E877 S44 2009 2009930895
[Fic]--dc22 0910

Printed in the USA
2 4 6 8 9 7 5 3 1

I dedicate this book to my husband, Mike, and our two daughters,
Christina and Bethany. You have taught me so much about love and life
and have journeyed with me through many storms on the Sea of Life.
I pray that you maintain always your allegiance to the
King of the Other Kingdom and keep your sails set
toward that better land.

Table of Contents

Acknowledgments

Writing the first three *Journey* books has been an exciting experience for me. I could not have done it without the encouragement of my husband, Mike, who took a huge load of other work off my shoulders so that I could stay on task.

There have been many encouragers who have added their thoughts to mine, believed in me, and expressed their confidence that these books will make a difference in the lives of readers everywhere.

I'd like to thank my editors, mentors, and colleagues who helped me through the process of birthing each of the three books in the *Book of Journeys* series, and especially Edict House editor Karla Wachenheim, who invested her heart as well as her time in this book. I can't say enough about your patience, persistence, and diligence in working with me to see this project through.

Cast of Characters

Addar (\ə-där\'): Emperor over all the worlds and father of Immon, also called the Dreadful One.

Immon (\i-män\'): King of the Other Kingdom, under his father, Addar, and rightful ruler over the Kingdom of Adawm (which includes all other kingdoms, including the City of Bondage and the Land of Lasciviousness). He died on the Hill of Death at the Cape of Conviction in order to purchase Certificates of Redemption for citizens of the Kingdom of Adawm.

The Messenger: Emissary of both Addar and Immon. He carries out their will in the Kingdom of Adawm, and travels with each person who pursues the quest for the Other Kingdom.

Grace: Friend of Addar and Immon, and the friend of those who dwell in Adawm.

Brae (Brā): Mikhail's friend from the First Book of Journeys, who preceded him to the shores of the Other Kingdom.

Mikhail (mi-kāl): A merchant sailor who became a friend to Brae.

Anastasia (an-as-tā-sha): Mikhail's wife.

Salina (\sə'-lē-nə\): Friend of the Messenger.

Sodomon (sô'-də-môn): Chief ruler over the Land of Lasciviousness, subject only to Dagog.

Dagog (dā'-gog): Usurper who dwells in the Middle Clouds, who rules the Kingdom of Adawm by violence and fear, and who is called by many names, including the Prince of the Darkness, the Dark Prince, and the Dark Presence. His pleasure is to steal, to kill, and to destroy everything that Addar treasures, especially the citizens of the Kingdom of Adawm, whom Addar created in his own image.

Wists: Servants of Dagog, near-human creatures who were alive and then dead and are now both dead and alive.

Whelter: Servants of Dagog in many varieties. Green-backed whelter (called the "rattler species") inject their victims with poison that kills instantly and are usually employed in direct combat. Purple, fluorescent green, and yellow whelter secrete venom that gradually paralyzes their victims, robbing them of sensitivity to danger until they are completely powerless and ready to be destroyed. Purple whelter are frequent objects of ridicule in the Middle Clouds.

Lucacius (lu-sā'-shus): An enormous wolven, Dagog's second in command.

Author's Note

The Book of Journeys *Series*

Seeking: The First Book of Journeys is somewhat of an allegory, though not in the strictest sense of the word. I have tried to communicate precious truths concerning salvation, deliverance, mercy, hope, and grace through the pages of *Seeking*. I hope those who are new to such concepts will better comprehend the good news of the gospel conveyed through the adventures of young Brae, former citizen of the City of Bondage, and his interactions with characters whose intentions are, in some cases, motivated by love, and in other cases, motivated by a desire to destroy him.

Experienced travelers on the Sea of Life, those who have made the acquaintance of the Messenger, Addar, and Immon, and become their friend, will enjoy revisiting the truths manifested in the Book of Journeys, in the same way that they may enjoy revisiting precious landmarks along their own path to the Other Kingdom.

Who among us would not take great pleasure in retracing the steps of our Lord Jesus Christ to the site of the tomb from which he arose? Who among us would disdain taking a trip down memory lane to the site of our own conversion beneath the spreading branches of "the silver birch tree"? Reminders of past joys may even alleviate present sufferings when life leads us along paths that are dark and unfamiliar.

I hope you will read each of the journey books and enjoy them as much as I have enjoyed writing them. I hope, also, that you will read these stories to small children, and encourage older children and adults to read the books themselves. Above all, I hope that these tales will encourage every reader to embark on his or her own journey to the Other Kingdom.

Introduction

This is the story of a quest—a quest that began when a certain slave boy, born in the City of Bondage, set out to escape from his cruel master. If he had known the perils he would encounter along the way, the awful fate that would be his if he fell into the clawed hand of Dagog, Prince of the Darkness, he might have remained in the City of Bondage. Perhaps he would have suffered less. Perhaps others in his city who knew better than he the horrors of Dagog's hatred should have warned the boy that there are miseries worse than slavery. Perhaps he would still be there today.

CHAPTER ONE:

The Journey Begins

No one noticed the freckle-faced youth who stood beside the merchant's table, peering over piles of pottery and bright bolts of fabric. His straw-colored hair seemed to have a mind of its own, sticking up like fresh-tossed hay in every direction. His green eyes squinted into the glare of the noonday sun.

"Where is the Messenger?" Brae was growing impatient. He had been told that the emissary of the great King Immon would come to the City of Bondage and that he would have the power to free the slaves of Meriquoi. Every day, as Brae took his place in the kiosk, counting change and wrapping the purchases of Meriquoi's customers, Brae watched and waited. Every beating he endured beneath Meriquoi's whip, every kick from his polished boot, made him long for the Messenger to come.

Brae slunk into the shadows, keeping a keen eye on the crowd moving restlessly along the dirt road that wound like a frayed ribbon through the congested marketplace.

The crowd parted, flowing away from a man who stood a head taller than those around him. The man exuded confidence, from the crown of his silver-gray hair to the tip of his shiny black boots. His golden-brown eyes seemed quick and alert beneath neatly trimmed brows that were the same color as his shoulder-length hair. His uniform, lined on the breast with a double row of buttons, complemented the stranger's military bearing.

Curious stares turned toward the stranger and then downward. Brae noticed that most of the citizens of the city seemed reluctant to meet his gaze. He paid them no heed as his long strides carried him swiftly toward the kiosk where Brae stood partially hidden behind bolts of cloth stacked high on the table.

Could this be the Messenger? Brae wondered. *Never have I seen one of his bearing in the City of Bondage.*

Disdaining the curious glances of the disorderly crowd, the stranger moved easily along, his eyes wide, scanning the kiosks that lined the congested, dusty road.

He is searching for me! Brae thought, his heart racing. Stepping out of the shadows, he stared boldly at the stranger. The Messenger nodded at Brae and moved on, small puffs of dust rising with each footfall.

Quickly, Brae slipped away from the kiosk and blended into the crowd, following a few feet behind the stranger. Brae's breath came in short gasps as he raced to keep up with the long paces of the Messenger.

With a start, Brae realized they had turned a corner and were heading toward the shipyard. "Am I to become a stowaway on one of the merchant ships anchored in the harbor?" Brae's hopes plummeted into despair.

I know what will happen to me if I am caught, he thought, and misery clutched at his throat like an iron fist.

Meriquoi will show no mercy. Brae tried not to think of other slaves who had attempted escape. Meriquoi knew well how to make an example of anyone who dared defy him. Meriquoi's skill with the whip was well known in the City of Bondage; he could flay the flesh from a slave's back and put him back to work a week later.

I will probably be reassigned to Jamie's job, Brae fretted. His misery escalated as he imagined himself carrying the sloppy chamber pots across the polished floors of Meriquoi's elegant house.

Stuffing his clenched fists into the pockets of his tattered, ankle-length pants, Brae kept walking, barely aware of the burning sand on his bare feet.

Turning, the Messenger beckoned the boy to follow him across a short, narrow bridge onto the deck of a small ship. It bore the name *Seeking.* The sun glistened on the varnished mahogany decking. Weathered masts reached for the clouds above the emerald waters of the bay. Somehow the ship, rocking in the gentle swells, seemed friendly.

Quickly, before his fearful thoughts could force him to return to the momentary safety of the kiosk, Brae stepped onto the deck and looked around. "Where am I to hide?"

The Messenger seemed surprised. "You do not hide aboard the good ship *Seeking*, my son." The Messenger paused, and then, as if bestowing a gift upon the terrified boy, he smiled. "You are under the protection of the great King Immon."

"King Immon..." Brae rolled the name slowly off his tongue. "King of the Other Kingdom?" Brae knew that he but parroted the words of Belita; he had little knowledge of the great king other than what Teller of Stories had imparted to him.

"Yes. This ship is in his service. If you depart these shores in the *Seeking*, you declare that you seek a country whose founder and royal governor is the great King Immon."

Brae hesitated. Suddenly aware of his rags he took a step backward, mistaking the insignificance of his stature in the Kingdom of Adawm and the fierce inferiority of his birth for an indisputable fact.

The Messenger shook his head and reached out to grasp the faltering boy's shoulder in his firm hand. "You err as do others who have begun to realize the power and greatness of the great king without having met him," he said, as if reading Brae's mind. "Even those who meet him often judge him by the lies they have been taught rather than the truths he so evidently demonstrates to them."

"But what if this King Immon will not allow me to enter his country?"

The Messenger nodded, conceding his point. "You are not yet ready to live in the Other Kingdom, Brae, for doubt rules in your heart. But the journey on the Sea of Life is long, and you will have opportunity to decide what you will do before you meet the great king.

Brae stared hard at the Messenger. Something about him reminded the boy of the Teller of Stories, who had entered the house of Meriquoi when Brae was a child of six summers. Patting the place on the rough plank floors before the stone fireplace in the slave quarters, she had smiled at Brae, and he had crept like an abandoned puppy, wary of her kindness, to her side. He had leaned against her and listened to her stories night after night. She told of the great King Immon and of his father, the Emperor Addar, Supreme Ruler of Kingdoms. "Addar is a mighty warrior," she had said, "yet he is as gentle as a lamb with his own children, especially his beloved son Immon." She had spoken tenderly, almost as if she spoke of her own son, as she wove a verbal tapestry of love and suffering, joy and anguish that seemed too good to be true, and simultaneously too precious on the lips of the Teller of Stories to be false.

The Messenger looked away from Brae, a grim expression, like the darkening clouds of an imminent storm crossing his face. "The Kingdom awaits you, Brae, but there is not time for delay. Will you go or do you choose to stay?"

Brae followed the Messenger's gaze, and terror, like the breaking of an angry sea, washed over him, for a cloud of dust rose from the pounding of feet along the road as twenty angry men raced toward the bay. Leading the pack was Meriquoi—his saber in his hand, wild eyes glazed, crooked teeth bared, like a tiger bereft of his prey.

There was no turning back! Brae nodded to the Messenger. "Yes! I will go."

The Messenger loosed the mooring ropes and began unfurling the sails, motioning to Brae to take the wooden wheel and guide the ship out of the bay.

Brae stared at the mob swarming toward the ship. Terror glued his feet to the planked deck, his throat tightened into a twisted knot, and his knees began to buckle as the angry men drew near.

"Brae!" The Messenger spoke sharply.

Brae leapt into action. He grabbed the wheel, feeling the ship glide away from the dock. The sails unfurled, instantly catching the sudden gust of wind that sprang out of nowhere, pushing the *Seeking* beyond the reach of Meriquoi.

The dark face of Brae's former master was crimson in his rage and scrunched like a sun-dried prune as he stood, half squatting in his fury. His heavy lips were mouthing words that Brae could easily imagine. Brae was glad he could not hear the profanities spewing from them as the stretch of water widened between the ship and those who shook their fists at heaven in impotent rage.

The wheel of the *Seeking* felt strange in the hands of the former slave boy from the City of Bondage. The sea, foaming above the swells, stretched to meet the salty blue horizon. The *Seeking* slipped over a hefty swell and dipped into a trough, rising quickly to catch the ridge of another swell and raise its prow toward the flaming white light high in the sky. In his anxiety, Brae imagined the *Seeking* was a great bird whose pinions spread across the waters to carry him into grave danger on uncharted seas.

Brae stared hard at the man who leaned upon the rail just a few feet from where he stood torn by doubt. Brae leaned on the rail at the port side of the ship and spit the bitterness from his mouth. Life in the City of Bondage was hard, but Brae wondered if he had merely traded a familiar misery for an unfamiliar one.

What have I done? he worried, as the City of Bondage faded in the distance. *I don't know this man. Even if there is a Messenger, somewhere, who will come someday, what if this man is not him? What if he is a slaver, or worse, one of the Mystics from the deep, wrapped in the flesh of man?* Brae had heard stories of such deceivers from the lips of hardened sailors who swore that these mystics sailed the seas in search of simple youths who could be captured and forced into their service. The mystics were charged with terrible, horrible, crimes, but were never tried because they simply evaporated into the mist when apprehended.

Brae's stomach felt as if a cauldron of fear boiled inside him. The hope that had given him courage to step out of the shadows and follow this stranger was lost among the anxieties that threatened to spill over to stain the gleaming deck of the *Seeking*.

Stop the ship! the slave boy thought, but did not say it. The *Seeking* sped on the wings of the wind toward a destination unknown to the boy, who stood with his gaze fastened on his deliverer, as if paralyzed by the chaos that coursed through his veins. Words, like blows from an invisible tormentor, hammered away at the hope buried deep within his heart.

Brae studied the face of the man who promised him freedom. This stranger was asking Brae to trust him. Trust did not come easily to one who had seldom known kindness. Brae had survived by being alert—always watchful, always ready to react when things went wrong.

But this stranger—this Messenger—seemed kind. The eyes that stared into Brae's were confident, mysterious. *Almost,* Brae thought, *like the eyes of Belita, the Teller of Stories.* The boy trembled as he remembered the hope that often rose in his heart as he sat before the dying embers of the evening fires, already dreading the cold that would creep into his bones when he climbed the narrow stairway to the attic cubbyhole that he called home. By night he listened to the words of Belita, by day he endured the pain, the humiliation, and the threats of Meriquoi; and that which he had believed in the night seemed but the fancies of an old woman in the light of day. And so he vacillated between hope and despair; between invisible truths and daily disappointments that threatened to drag him into the muck of resignation, committing him forever to slavery in the City of Bondage.

Not all the slaves of Meriquoi were pleased when Belita spoke of the Messenger. Some were angry, displeased that anyone should challenge their complacency.

"I will believe it when I see it!" a thin youth muttered. His back was crisscrossed with the scars of many beatings, his fists clenched at his sides.

"No," Belita had said. "You will see it, my son, when you can believe it."

At first Brae too thought Belita spoke the foolishness of an old woman, one who dreamed too much. But she was so confident, so certain that Immon would send his Messenger to those who called out to him—those who refused to be silenced—that Brae dared to hope, perhaps even to believe that life existed somewhere beyond the City of Bondage. He began to believe that somehow, someday, he could be free. When he began to doubt, Belita always knew. She would chide, "Do not fear, young Brae! One day you will see!"

How strong she was. *But not strong enough.* Brae's eyes filled with tears and he blinked, ashamed to cry in the presence of the stranger who stood beside him, watching, waiting, somehow, it seemed, *knowing* that even though he stood aboard the *Seeking* he was not yet committed to the journey.

The Messenger's face became solemn. "There is one thing that you must know. Immon has an enemy. He is called, Dagog, Prince of the Darkness. He is lord over the evil master whom you have served from your birth, and lord over all the Kingdom of Adawm. If you leave these shores, he will do all that is in his power to destroy you."

"But he cannot, right?" Brae asked hopefully. "I mean, if I am under the protection of Immon—"

"Immon promises you life in the Other Kingdom, Brae. "He does not say that you will not suffer. For it is impossible for anyone to enter into that fair land without having suffered in this one."

Returning the firm gaze of the Messenger, Brae felt his doubt and fears melt away like butter beneath the burning rays of the sun, and resolve hardened his words. "I would rather die trying to escape than live any longer in the City of Bondage."

Brae felt older than his seventeen years as he leaned into the wind. He glanced back at the city. It was the only home he had ever known.

Home. He shrugged. There is no home for a slave.

Brae turned away from the City of Bondage determined that he would never again look back. As he did so, a shadow passed over the *Seeking*. Brae gasped and peered into the clouds. There was nothing in the sky but pale blue space, white clouds, and a couple of seagulls. Nothing more.

"It is Dagog, Prince of the Darkness." The Messenger was grim.

At these words, Brae became aware of the smell of sulfur. The sea seemed to be shrouded in a strange gray mist, though the sun blazed upon the water as brightly as before. Brae wondered if the mist was real or only a figment of his imagination.

At the sound of huge wings flapping lazily against the currents of the sky, Brae's courage failed, and he looked at the water, measuring the distance to shore. The angry mob had dispersed. *No one would notice if I slipped back into the city,* he thought. *Perhaps I could change my appearance, assume a different name. I could find a place on one of the islands near the city, where I could work for the fishermen. They always need boys to mend their nets, scrub their boats.*

A squat, powerful figure returned to the dock, his right hand on his sheathed saber, his left shielding his eyes from the glare of the sun as he stared across the deep blue waters of the bay. *Even if the man on the dock is Meriquoi, there is no way he can reach across the waves to capture me,* Brae reasoned. Such logic did little to abate the terror that threatened to emasculate the runaway slave.

The man on the dock turned away and left the shipyard, but Brae's troubled thoughts kept spinning. *I could still slip back into the city. I am a strong swimmer.... But what if I am discovered? What if someone recognizes me and reports me to Meriquoi? The Messenger may not come this way again; there will be no way of escape.*

The Messenger was silent. A seagull chattered overhead. Waves slapped at the sides of the ship. The hot sun shimmered on the water. Once again, Brae looked into the eyes of the Messenger and was reminded of the only true friend he had ever known. He turned to look across the open water that stretched to infinity before him and noted the dragon-like shadow that draped itself across the waves, rising and falling on the cresting seas. Dagog, it seemed, would stalk him to the ends of the earth. *Well,* Brae thought, *Belita never said the journey would be easy and it is obvious now that it is also dangerous.*

Brae clenched the wheel with both hands and faced the horizon, glad that the Messenger was at his side as he fled the City of Bondage and began his journey on the Sea of Life.

Chapter Two:

The Ancient Book of Mysteries

Brae studied the ancient manuscripts, charts, and maps in the captain's quarters as he followed the rising sun. He was intrigued by one especially large volume called *The Ancient Book of Mysteries.* The front of the brown leather tome was adorned with the picture of a silver birch tree. A thick trunk, somewhat gnarled by time and perhaps by the abuse of battles fought beneath its silvered canopy, occupied the center of the cover.

Belita had loved "the tree." Her voice always dropped in pitch and grew soft when she spoke of it. Brae had felt as he had when watching a tender love scene in one of the many dramas presented for all to see on the streets of the City of Bondage. Even in the city, the love of a man for a maiden was sometimes portrayed as a pure and beautiful mystery.

Late one evening, Brae sat on his bed, opened the *Book of Mysteries*, and propping the thick volume on his lap, began to read. The letters were strange to him, though beautiful, with graceful curves and flowing endings that made him feel as if he were entering the private world of an author whose scholarship and authority marked him for a great and noble dignitary. Embarrassed and somewhat intimidated by his intrusion into what he now perceived to be a collection of private letters by this unknown person, Brae felt that he should close the book. But he found it impossible to do so.

The candle burned low as Brae turned the pages. The words meant little to him for their meaning seemed far beyond his understanding. But the illustrations, they were a different matter.

There were pictures of battles fought by men with swords and armor. Sometimes they fought human foes and the blood ran thick and red. In other pictures, they fought creatures so grotesque and horrible that Brae quickly turned the pages.

At some point, Brae realized with a start that the candle had burned out. The pages of the *Ancient Book* were illuminated by a light from within, a soft golden glow. Brae quickly closed the book and backed away from the bed, afraid to touch the strange volume.

He pulled his blanket off the end of the bed and wrapped himself in it on the floor. The gentle roll of the *Seeking* and the soft moaning of the wind through the rigging comforted him, as a child rocked in his mother's arms, though Brae had never experienced a mother's love. He fell into the embrace of the night with a deep sigh and an aching in his heart that he could not understand as loneliness paid him an unexpected visit. He longed for something, or someone, but did not know who or what. Longing became an ache in his heart, as hunger is an ache in the belly when one has been long deprived of food.

The stars grew dim as the morning light diffused the darkness. Still, Brae slept, dreaming of battles and monsters and strange lights that illuminated his room and penetrated his flesh, condensing finally somewhere inside him, a presence that soothed his loneliness and filled, ever so slightly, a cavernous void in a chamber in which a single piece of furniture rocked back and forth.

In the days that followed, Brae thought often of the *Ancient Book*. He had returned it to its place on the rich mahogany desk that occupied a corner of his room. Sometimes, on the darkest of nights, he would awaken and notice that the silver birch tree glowed softly in the darkness.

Strangely, Brae felt both compelled and repelled by the warm golden light. Compelled to open the book and allow himself to be drawn into its pages, to become a part of the history written there; but at the same time repelled by the sacrifice that he intuitively understood such a decision would require of him. Brae had fled the tyranny of Meriquoi but he had taken the City of Bondage with him in his heart.

The Messenger was not deceived. "You have to let it go," he said to Brae one day as they sat at the table in the galley.

"What?" Brae asked, startled. His mind had wandered back to the city, reliving one of the many lewd festivals that had entertained and tantalized him. Feeling guilty, but also amazed at the Messenger's uncanny ability to know what he was thinking; Brae became angry. "I don't know what you're talking about!" he said.

The Messenger stood and walked up the steps to the rail. A brisk wind billowed the sails of the *Seeking*. Brae followed the Messenger up the stairs to the poop and took the wheel. Roiling black clouds hung low over the horizon and rain began to pelt the rising waves. Night came early without stars or moon. The *Seeking* rose on the crest of each dark wave and crashed into the foaming trough between the swells.

Brae was glad for the rain, for it masked the tears that trailed down his face as he stood at the wheel alone in the dark and the storm.

Chapter Three:

Doubt Breeds Despair

The following day dawned clear and bright. The air smelled as fresh and clean as sun-dried laundry. Brae leaned against the rail, his eyes closed, remembering.

He was a little boy of about seven or eight years and had been assigned the task of helping Belita take care of Meriquoi's laundry. He took each fine cotton garment, still damp from the washing, out of the wicker basket and shook it out, handing it to Belita, who fastened it to the wire line that stretched across a hidden alcove in Meriquoi's estate.

Once again, longing created an agonizing ache in Brae's chest as he remembered the tropical paradise of Meriquoi's gardens. He could smell the fruity fragrance of blood-red bromeliads with their evergreen fans, feel the shade of white bird of paradise with its dark green leaves and bright yellow fruit. Cool breezes swept across the enormous fountain centered with a bronze sculpture of the entwined bodies of sensuous naked couples performing the rites of passage into adult life.

"Brae." The voice of the Messenger interrupted Brae's journey into the past, a place already changing in the young man's mind, metamorphosing into something that it was not—paradise without pain. "You need to remember the pain."

"Why?" Brae's face flushed with anger. "Why can't I just forget all that and keep the good memories?"

"Because it is the Truth that sets you free, Brae, and distorted truths are only lies masquerading as reality."

"So what? What if they are lies? If my lies make me happy, why should you care?"

"Because happiness built on lies will crumble into ashes, but Truth will plant the seeds of joy that will endure through the tempest of time. Get to know the Truth, Brae, for Truth alone can set you free."

Brae turned on his heel and stalked to his room. He threw himself on his bed, refusing to glance in the direction of the *Ancient Book of Mysteries*. The silver birch tree with its gentle illumination mocked him now.

Another storm broke across the horizon and Brae went on deck to look into the sky. A strange dark cloud, shaped like a bird with a beaked reptilian head, stretched across the canvas of the sky. A lighter mist of dirty gray splayed across the space beyond it, and the smell of sulfur hung heavy on the wet, cold air.

Brae shivered. "It is just a cloud," he spoke aloud as he crossed the deck to take the wheel of the *Seeking*. Doubt, like an invisible bandit, blinded his eyes and whispered questions in his ear.

"Do you really think an Other Kingdom exists?" the throaty whisper, almost a growl, neither surprised nor intimidated Brae. It seemed natural and somehow familiar.

Belita was certain that it did. Brae thought, remembering the faraway expression on her face when she talked about the Other Kingdom, as if she could see through some invisible doorway into a different world.

Brae blinked back tears, remembering the ship that brought Belita to the shores of his city. The *Scavenger* was owned by a ruthless merchant whose teeth were capped with gold, his one eye squeezed into a perpetual squint. His other eye had been, so they said, pierced by the spear of an angry boy whose father lay squirming in the net of the slavers along with a dozen of his neighbors—ambushed at the village council and then herded like cattle into the bowels of the *Scavenger.*

Some said that Belita was the wife of one of the men, that she clung to his arm and was dragged along with the others to the *Scavenger* and thrown into the hold.

She had stood on the slave block staring into the ripped clouds, heavy and dark against the heavens. She had refused to watch as all the men from her village were led away, bound by a common rope, and forced to board another ship, the *Scabbard*, bound for unknown lands far away.

Left alone, Belita shed no tears. She did not struggle as Meriquoi paid the slaver a meager price and laid a rough hand on her shoulder, pushing her along the dusty road to his house as if she was a thing that could be bought! The more Meriquoi mistreated her, the kinder she became, like a ripe piece of fruit that became sweeter with the bruising.

Though the rain continued to drizzle, the sun came out from behind the clouds, and beacons of light shone like golden cones upon the face of the sea.

Brae shook his head. *What is getting into me? I am not even sure the Other Kingdom exists; and if it does, I am not certain that I want to go there.* Brae felt anger rise in his heart.

Belita was my friend—but she was a slave, like me. If there is an Other Kingdom, and if the king of that Kingdom is a great and powerful ruler... Brae slammed his fist down on the wooden wheel. *Then why... why did her king let her die?*

Sadness and rage swept through him. Sorrow buried beneath the helpless despair of seventeen years of bondage rose to the surface as oil rises in water as he sailed through warm sunshine and cool cleansing rains.

This bitter episode was followed abruptly by a guilty conscience as Brae conceded that *someone* had sent the Messenger in the *Seeking* to deliver him from the bloody hands of Meriquoi. Still, Belita's kind, benevolent king seemed incongruent with the disinterested sovereign who would allow his faithful subject to be mutilated by the likes of Meriquoi.

Chapter Four:

The Assignment

Dagog was comfortable in his favorite element. The roiling black clouds pierced occasionally by violent electrical spears soothed him, for turmoil was his delight. Seated upon a mountain of smoky cloud, he crossed his legs and folded his wings at his sides. His students, the most elite class from the realm of the living-dead, sat in a semicircle around him. They did not love their teacher, for none of them was capable of this or any other noble emotion, but they admired him, in fact, they worshipped him. This was evident in the bowed heads and submissive glances they offered their teacher and master.

"I have an assignment for one of you," the beast began. "There has been... a deserter in the Kingdom of Adawm. A slave boy by the name of Brae has fled the shores of the City of Bondage." The sound of grinding teeth and sucked-in breath, such as was expected, mingled with the rumble of thunder. "I have... concerns. Every citizen of the kingdom that leaves our ranks and aligns himself with the Dreadful One will win others to His side. Apparently, my students have not all learned, as well as you, the art of deception."

At these words of flattery, the bowed heads of Dagog's subjects bent even lower until it appeared that their heads would snap right off their necks. Dagog smiled, not a pleasant sight, for there was no affection in it.

"Umbler!" He called upon a junior dragon who, of all his subjects, looked the most like himself. "You are in charge of the deserter who travels aboard the *Seeking* with the... the..." Dagog, as usual, had a hard time speaking the name of the Messenger. He hated him, but could not deny a certain admiration for one superior in every way to himself. His subjects understood and wisely decided to nod their agreement, ignoring this small weakness on the part of their master. "You must persuade him to forsake the journey on which he has embarked."

Umbler knelt before Dagog and received his charge. "Do not fail me!" Dagog thundered and the heavens cringed before his foul breath. He did not have to expound upon his threat, for all his subjects trembled, knowing already that Umbler was not truly fortunate to be chosen for this task. They, one and all, were secretly relieved not to have been chosen for this honor.

Umber, who like Dagog, was a form changer, asked, "Do I have your permission, oh Great Master, to use all means at my disposal to assure our success?"

"You must." Dagog answered, for he knew that along with the seeds of doubt his subjects had sown in Brae's young heart, seeds of hope had been sown by the woman who loved him as her own son. He grimaced at this, consoled only by the memory of the punishment meted out to the student who had failed to conquer the woman named Belita.

As the meeting adjourned, Umber sailed the currents of the sky under the black canopy of night, plotting the destruction of one who had escaped the shores of the City of Bondage but had not yet surrendered his allegiance to the king of the Other Kingdom.

"This is the time to get him!" Umbler exulted, enjoying the caress of darkness against his scaled body. Obsessed with his plans, he bumped into a star and fell through the sky, landing with a splash upon his bottom. He found it difficult to think for a few days due to the pounding ache in his head, so it took him awhile to make his first move.

Chapter Five:

The Port of Plenty

Days passed into weeks, and the supply of food and water aboard the *Seeking* dwindled. The wind howling over the Sea of Life grew cold and sharp, nipping at the exposed flesh on Brae's elbows and legs. His shoulders hunched against the gale, Brae shivered in his rags. Meriquoi cared not that his slaves were cold and underfed. The tattered shirt and the thin fabric in the short pants that covered Brae gave little protection from the weather.

Brae was huddled into a corner, wishing for his old room in the attic in the City of Bondage, when he saw smoke rising into the white clouds. He scrambled to the rail and saw that the *Seeking* was approaching land. A wooden sign anchored in the sand bore the words Port of Plenty.

The Messenger laid a hand on Brae's arm. "Do not forget that you are in search of the Other Kingdom." His kind eyes looked concerned. "You will find danger even in the Port of Plenty."

The Messenger began furling the sails, and Brae prepared to drop anchor. As the ship drifted into the shelter of the harbor, Brae launched a small boat and rowed hard toward the Port of Plenty, his eyes fixed upon the shore. Had he looked up, he would have seen the winged monster that glided through the fleece of clouds above his head. If he had seen the streak of crimson that trailed behind the creature, bleeding into a pink-tinged column and then dissipating in the faint blush of the near-setting sun, Brae would have spun the small craft around and rowed back to the *Seeking* as fast as he could. If he had looked to the starboard side of his craft, he would have seen the dark reptilian shadow on the water. He might have been spared the sorrows that would soon befall him at the Port of Plenty.

The sharp eyes of The Messenger, watching from the rail of the *Seeking*, squinted into the wounded sky and grieved for the boy who approached the shoreline of the Port of Plenty, ignorant of the injury that may befall one who accepts such bounty without recognizing its Source.

A few children played in the sand beneath the weathered sign that bore the name of the village. They shouted when they saw Brae. Men and women came running, their faces wreathed in smiles, their voices excited. "Welcome," they said, "to the Port of Plenty."

Brae smiled back, holding out his hands to the children, who grabbed him and tried to drag him toward a great fire in the village square. The villagers prepared a feast, piling a wooden table high with fresh meat and steaming corn, potatoes, and fried cakes dipped in honey. As the sun slipped out of sight beneath the flaming waters, Brae patted his full stomach and strolled over to the fire to sit cross-legged on the ground beside a muscular young man whom he later learned was the son of Anthar, governor of the Port of Plenty. He warmed his back at the fire, content to sit there, listening to the chatter of the women, the blustering of the young men, and the squealing laughter of children.

The night grew cold and mothers carried their children off to bed. A few old men told outrageous tales about visitors who had come to the Port of Plenty in times past.

A toothless crone with stick thin legs and gray hair knotted into a kerchief at the nape of her wrinkled neck listened as if paying little attention to the ramblings of men who had outlived their purpose and now spent their days reinventing the past.

A full moon high overhead silvered the sandy shore and the lush palms that bordered the port city. Brae glanced at the good ship *Seeking* bobbing on the gentle swells in the dark waters of the harbor.

There is a certain... mystery about the old ship, he thought. A twinge of longing stirred somewhere deep down inside him, so far down—beneath the joy of unfamiliar pleasures—that Brae hardly noticed it at all. Then it passed, and he was glad to have his feet planted on the good earth. His eyes began to droop. The voices droning on and on had grown dim, when something startled him wide-awake.

It was the voice of the old crone, speaking in a singsong voice.

There's others that's come this way before
To mend their boat and refill their stores
They gave us more than they took from us
And the King of the Kingdom of Adawm—it was
That sent them here and give us the heart
To fill us their boats and to do our part
To get them along on their merry way
To the Other Kingdom without delay.
But those that comes to take our best
With their own uncaring selfishness
A curse I say! A double one too
And if you don't like it—a curse on you!
There's foul a foot, I seen the beast
Flying high in the sky when we was at feast.
Happy he's not, trouble is sure
He's heading I think for the Valley of E'ure
Where once a time, yes, long ago
He was beat at his game, but doesn't know
So after this boy, I am sure that he is
For the King has called, but it is not yet His,
Safe it is not, this boy from the ship
For the folk in the port are no matter to it
Sleeping away the last of the night
If you listen to me you will send it a-flight
Trouble will come an' I say it ain't long
For this boy—it ain't no friend of Immon.

Brae opened one eye just a tiny bit, hoping his long lashes would conceal the fact that he was not sleeping, but searching for the speaker. Then he saw her. The old woman was rocking back and forth as if swaying to inaudible music, chanting the words through wrinkled lips, eyes wide like a cadaver's staring straight ahead. Her thin fingers raked the air, her long black talons curving around an invisible object known only to her. She reached out her bony arms and drew them back in a swimming motion. She was still caught up in her own private drama when the old men got up, one by one, shaking their heads, and turned from the fire to retire, each to his own house.

Alone with the old woman, Brae found it impossible to keep up the pretense of sleep, so he sat up, rubbing his eyes as if just awakened.

"Humph!" the woman said, getting to her feet and abruptly turning her back on him. She walked away without a word and Brea sat trembling before the dying fire, glad that the night was almost over.

Within minutes, dawn broke across the horizon and the morning sky burst into flames of gold and crimson. Dew drenched palms glistened black against the breaking day, fading slowly in the brightening sun to shades of charcoal gray. Their verdant foliage swept the sky like lazy fingers in the early breeze. Dogs barked. The village was waking.

CHAPTER SIX:

A Journey Forsaken

After breakfast the governor sent his servant to lead Brae to a house at the edge of the village. Surrounded by lazy palms and pink bromeliads, the lawn stretched to the white sands that met the emerald sea. Brae's breath caught in his throat. Does this mean that I am to live here? he thought, amazed at his good fortune.

Two women, hardly older than he, stood in the doorway, eagerly awaiting his approval. Brae entered and looked around at the clean, well-appointed dwelling and nodded his thanks. One of the women handed him a stack of soft woolen blankets and a strange object that he had never seen before.

"What is this?" He held up the long stick, which had bristles, like the hair of a wild hog, fastened in its end.

The women looked at each other and giggled. One of them took it from his hand and began to brush her hair with it. Handing it back to him, she stepped outside, stifling laughter until she and her companion were out of sight.

Brae crossed the room to sit on the bed. It was filled with goose down, soft as a pillow. Bright rugs adorned the planed wooden floor. The fragrance of orchids permeated the room. *If only Belita could see me now,* Brae thought, his chest swelling with pride. *Never has a slave of Meriquoi enjoyed such luxury.*

Autumn yielded to winter, and winter to spring. Still Brae lingered in the Port of Plenty. He no longer looked toward the sea. He tried to forget that the Messenger waited aboard the *Seeking.* He refused to think of the Messenger's warning. He could see no danger here. The Messenger could go on waiting.

Brae spent most of the day lying in the hammock that swung between two trees or playing with the children in the sand. He chose to ignore the disdain of the young men who glanced his way as they did their work, the women talking behind their hands. He looked away from the baleful stares of the governor's eldest son, Jiron, whose house now belonged to Brae. *Anthar remains friendly,* Brae thought, *so why should I care?*

One summer day when the sun shimmered on the waves and the rhythm of the surf lulled even the most active child to nap in the shade, Brae lay in the hammock, dimly aware of a shadow that passed between the sun and his closed eyes.

He tried not to think of it, yet in the weeks that followed, he dreamed often of a long, dark shadow floating in grotesque distortions over swelling waves, accompanied always by the odor of sulfur that stung his nostrils. Strangely, the smell lingered long after sleep had fled and left Brae trembling in the dark.

One night, Brae was roused from a peaceful slumber. There was a quarter-moon and few stars, rendering the darkness thick and black. The sound of feet pounding along the dirt path outside his door aroused Brae further, just in time to see shadowy forms disappear into the forest, his belongings spilling from their hands.

Something fell in the house, making a loud noise against the wooden floor. Now fully awake, Brae saw shadowy forms in the darkness of his room. He heard quiet shallow breathing. Suddenly, angry hands grabbed him, their fingers clutching his hair. A voice hissed, "I am sick to death of you, lazy dog! What have you done to deserve my house, my food, and my father's favor?"

Blood pounded in Brae's ears, like the feathery beat of a giant winged creature. He almost believed he saw the shadow of a reptilian creature, a monster whose beaked head and talons strained toward him, reaching, clutching at him, as though they would curl themselves around his body and crush him as a vulture crushes the bones of a carcass.

Jiron motioned to someone standing outside. The door was thrown back against the wall, and four young men, all of them angry, all wielding wooden clubs, stormed into the room. Brae screamed and fell to the floor as the first blow struck. Blood stained the woven rug where he lay, his knees drawn up to his chest.

A dog barked, and someone shouted. The blows ceased. Quietly the young men left the house without a backward glance, all except Jiron. "Get out," he commanded. "If you are here at daybreak, you will not live another day."

In the thick darkness, haunted by the deeper darkness of shadows that loomed against the night, Brae left the Port of Plenty. Too weak to stand, he crawled, inching his way, one painful stretch at a time, toward the bay, leaving bloody prints to mark the path of his retreat.

He found the rowboat that had brought him to these shores where he had left it, beneath the low branches of a cypress outlined faintly against the still night.

The light of a lantern glowed from the deck of the *Seeking*. Brae kept his gaze on it, slowly pushing at the oars with the weight of his body.

Bitter tears burned his eyes as he thought of the warm blankets and baskets of food he had wasted in the Port of Plenty. Now he was returning to an empty ship. And he had no one to blame but himself. With little hope, he pushed again at the oars, but the outline of the ship was growing dimmer now, swimming in a misty haze. As Brae squinted into the distance, it slipped from his sight completely, and he lay motionless in the bottom of the boat, drifting, dreaming—vague, unconnected scenes that made no sense at all.

Thump. Thump. Brae became dimly aware of the sound. Reaching out, he found he was still slumped in the bottom of the rowboat. Blood soaked his torn clothing and matted his hair. His cheeks burned as saltwater doused raw abrasions. Peering through swollen eyes, he recognized the *Seeking*. He tried to stand, only to collapse against the bottom of the rowboat. He tried again, reaching desperate hands toward the *Seeking*, but his knees buckled, and he hit his head against the side of the boat as he sank back into it. The ship began to drift away. Brae's battered body shook with sobs.

As in a dream, he felt hands, small but strong, lifting him. Though he saw no one, he became dimly aware that he stood—with a strength not his own. He realized that the rowboat had moved forward once more to bump against the ship, where the Messenger stood at the rail, his hands extended.

Brae tried to reach his arms up, as a child reaches for his father, but found that there was no strength left in them. As the ship began to drift beyond his reach, he looked helplessly into the Messenger's kind face. Once again, he felt the hands of one he could not see lift up his arms and hold them fast, as the rowboat surged on the crest of a wave toward the ship. Finally, the Messenger's hands touched his, and Brae felt himself propelled from behind by an unseen presence and pulled gently aboard by the Messenger's strong hands.

As Brae struggled to stand on the deck, he looked around in disbelief. There, before his eyes, was an abundant supply of food and water. A stack of blankets lay nearby.

"While you delayed your return," the Messenger said, "Grace came and supplied all that you need to continue your journey."

Then Brae noticed the woman who had followed him out of the rowboat. She stood at the Messenger's side, her hand resting lightly on his arm. Her eyes were blue like the waters of the deep, her fair skin flawless. Her hair, reaching past her shoulders, shone like spun gold. A blue sash, reaching down to the hem of her long flowing dress, draped her small waist. Her eyes were warm with compassion as the wounded boy crumpled against the friend he had forgotten. The Messenger picked up a wool blanket and wrapped it around Brae's shoulders.

The moon was high among the stars when Brae fell asleep that night. As he slept, he dreamed that the Messenger visited a place that was far away and yet so near that he had merely to step into it, and that there he obtained a royal blue vase, trimmed with golden leaves and adorned with slender curved handles. Lifting it high, he poured a drop of golden oil onto the tip of his finger. Gently, he touched the oil to the suffering boy.

"By the wounds of the Wounded One, you are healed," he whispered. The Messenger looked at Brae, sleeping the sleep of one whose strength has departed. Tenderly, he applied another drop of the oil to the boy's wounds. "By his wounds..." he repeated. The boy's labored breathing grew quiet.

The Messenger climbed the stairs to the deck and stood at the railing, looking out into the night, remembering the horrible day.

The Wounded One was his friend. He walked and talked with him through the corridors of time. Always, he had known that he would slip out of the halls of the Other Kingdom and enter the Kingdom of Adawm. He had known that the Wounded One would suffer much, for the price of redemption would not be cheap.

Emperor Addar himself laid the plans before the dawn of time. He knew that he would suffer the agony of bereavement, as his own son, King of the Other Kingdom, exchanged his royal throne for the dusty paths in the Valley of E'ure—the place of sacrifice, the battlefield for the souls of mankind.

But knowing and experiencing are as different as the heat of the desert sun and the chill of the Arctic seas.

"I couldn't protect him," the Messenger lamented. "The Kingdom of Adawm was his treasure—and it was his choice to pay the price of its redemption. There was no other way."

Chapter Seven:

A Visit in the Night

The night yielded to a still greater darkness, an unnatural absence of light. The moon hid behind smoky clouds bunched together like chunks of charcoal in a cotton bag. Shadows, shaped like beasts raised from the pit—known only by legend and the occasional sighting by those who have come under their power—writhed, slithered, and thundered across the sky.

Umbler spread his leathery wings, callused by the ravages of time, delighting in the roar of thunder and the charge of electrical of energy that illuminated his fierce countenance for a fraction of a second. The wolven Lucacius, commander of Dagog's forces, loped along at Umbler's side, his fangs glistening in the lightning strokes from on high. His eyes were red as blood, his neck thick and shaggy. He threw back his enormous head and howled at the storm, exultant on this darkest of nights.

Whelter, snake-like creatures with the bloodsucking habits of the leech, attached themselves to the back of the wolven and the dragon and glowed like fireflies in the night. Some who watch the sky may have thought that they were aliens, and of course they would have been right, for such creatures were not created for this world.

The Messenger watched them whirl away through the clouds. He knew where they were going. Whenever a traveler on the Sea of Life lost his way, Dagog often met for council at the Valley of E'ure, the place of death. They went there to gloat, to boast of their victory in the very spot where Dagog had suffered his greatest defeat.

Suddenly, there was a flash of bright light. Dazzling and pure, it shone through the darkness. It looked, at first, like the beam of a beacon such as one might see at the top of a lighthouse, a light to guide lost boats to safety on a troubled sea; then it began to condense, growing smaller but brighter. Finally, it took the shape of a dove, larger than most, but beautifully formed. The light dimmed as it entered the dove and was diffused, becoming a soft warm glow shining from within the dove.

The white dove lifted its wings and sailed into the smoky sky. As it flew, the storm clouds dissipated and the stars began to shine. The moon peeked out and then rose above the clouds to light the sky and the sea beneath. Still the dove ascended. Breaking through the ranks of stars, it entered the realm of the Other Kingdom. The shining warriors bowed before him and a courier hastened to the throne room to announce his arrival. But the courier was too slow. Before he reached steps of the royal palace, the dove had entered, made straight for the throne room, and alighted on the arm of Immon, son of the Imperial Emperor Addar.

King Immon laughed at the courier whose astonished expression gave way to a delighted grin.

"Everyone likes to be the bearer of good news," Immon said. "You have done well, my friend, but General Minome may have better use of your services than I at the moment."

As the courier hastened away, Immon turned to the Dove resting lightly on his arm. He stroked the Dove's feathers and looked into its golden-brown eyes. He did not address the Dove directly, but those who stood by knew that he engaged the Dove in a long conversation, though no words were spoken. Between the Dove and Immon words were unnecessary for each knew the other's mind perfectly.

Emperor Addar, Imperial Ruler of Kingdoms, smiled. He, too, knew the language of the heart shared by Immon and the Dove. He laughed along with Immon when the Dove commented on the journey of Dagog to the Valley of E'ure. His eyes twinkled and he reached an enormous hand to clap the knee of Immon, "Will the beast never learn that his victories are as empty as the grave?"

Immon lifted his arm and the Dove took flight. It circled the thrones of Addar and Immon once, and again, and then it was gone. Within moments the Dove descended to the deck of the *Seeking*, where a former slave from the City of Bondage was just waking from a sound sleep.

CHAPTER EIGHT:

Umbler's Bright Idea

Umbler returned from the council in the Valley of E'ure with dragging wings. The meeting had not gone well. Dagog was incensed at the failure of the trap in the Port of Plenty, and took his frustration out on his most convenient subject.

Umbler rubbed his aching head and tried to ignore the pain in his injured wing. He had known this assignment would not be easy, but hadn't expected failure so soon.

Lucacius sat on his haunches across from the wounded dragon, grinning. He always enjoyed the failures of others. It was so inspiring. It made him feel... superior. His smug expression irritated the dragon.

"Well, don't you have anything to say?" Umbler squirmed.

"You want me to say I told you so?" Lucacius raised one bushy eyebrow and cocked his head to one side.

The dragon glared at his rival. "Dagog said you could give me some... pointers. This case is obviously not going according to our plan."

"Well..." Lucacius drawled, stretching the word as long as possible, "perhaps you should ask for assistance from someone more... suited to the task."

Had the wolven been flesh and blood he would have been disintegrated by the fiery glare of red-hot dragon eyes. But of course he was not and so he just grinned at the dragon, which exhaled a ferocious black cloud in his direction. Lucacius sniffed the air—sulfur. Delicious.

"I know just the right assistant for you." Lucacius suggested. "It takes a certain skill to succeed with the young ones. He will do the work and you will receive the credit."

The suggestion cheered the junior dragon. "Yes. You are exactly right, Commander." An ugly grin spread Umbler's face, extending from the blue-green mole on the left side of his crooked mouth to the blood-red wart that dangled, like a worm on a hook, from his right cheek. His headache faded and even his wounded wing felt a little better.

Chapter Nine:

A Perilous Companion

Young bones mend quickly, and it was not long before Brae was up and about. Soon he was diving into the sea for a swim, climbing the rigging in search of land, and becoming quite bored. One day, he was in the crow's nest, telescope in hand, when he spotted a raft approaching. He laughed at the sight of it, for it was purple. The young man inside was having the time of his life, waving his hat and yelling every time the boat rode a cresting wave, landing with a splash in the troughs. He was heading straight for the *Seeking*. Brae did not notice that the shadow cast across the waves by the boy did not fit his slender shape. Shadowed wings stretched wide across the foaming swells, cresting white like feathers shed by some great bird.

"Hey!" Brae shouted, cupping his hands over his mouth. "You, over there. Come aboard."

A friendly grin spread across the tan face of the youth in the purple boat. His long curly hair, black as soot, stirred in the morning breeze. Lifting his hand in a cocky salute, he squinted into the sun. "Sure," he called. "I'll be right there."

In a few moments, the stranger had pulled alongside, lightly scrambled up a rope ladder, and vaulted over the rail. He winked at the Messenger, who stood, frowning, at the rail, and advanced toward Brae, a grin on his face and his hand outstretched.

"Hi," he bubbled. "I'm Damon."

"I'm Brae. Welcome aboard."

Looking around the ship and sniffing the aroma of soup cooking, Damon said, "Ummm, something sure smells good."

Brae didn't wait for him to ask. "There's plenty," he said, looking at the Messenger for confirmation. The Messenger said nothing.

"Well, then." Brae ended the awkward silence. He clapped Damon on the shoulder. "Let's check out the galley."

Damon bent over the soup bubbling in the cast-iron pot, then opened the door of the oven. "Cornbread." He sounded like he had just struck gold. "Let's eat."

Both boys grabbed bowls and filled them to the brim. They scooped out chunks of red potatoes, squash, and tomatoes and heaped them onto plates.

"Hey," Brae grabbed Damon's hand, the first misgiving flitting like a startled bird across his thoughts. "Save some for the Messenger."

"Oh, I forgot about him," Damon said.

The meal was filled with laughter. Afterward, in no hurry to leave the table, Damon talked excitedly about all the fun he and Brae were going to have. He seemed oblivious to Brae's increasing discomfort about the Messenger waiting on deck for Brae to replace him at the wheel while the meager remnants of soup grew cold.

Finally, unable to sit still a minute longer, Brae jumped up and playfully punched Damon. "Hey, let's go on deck and you can take a turn at the wheel!"

"Let's go!" Damon grinned in reckless delight.

When Brae went to bed that night, he neglected to say goodnight to the Messenger. In fact, he tiptoed past the Messenger, sneaking down the narrow stairs to his bunk. The Messenger, staring out to sea, seemed not to notice. Brae wondered what he was thinking.

Long after Brae fell asleep, the Messenger kept his vigil. Damon knew the reason for his diligent watch, even if Brae did not. The moon rose high above the *Seeking*, casting its pale light upon the sea. The Messenger was aware of Damon's presence beside him at the rail. Still he waited for the deceiver to speak.

"I will win, you know." Damon's boyish voice had been discarded for this conversation. There was no need to pretend with the Messenger. His low growl would have made the hair stand up on Brae's neck if he could have heard it.

The Messenger did not bother to answer. Keeping his eyes fixed on the black water, he held the rail with a grip that whitened his knuckles.

"He doubts you already," the hoarse whisper prodded. "He is mine...."

At the last word, the Messenger turned toward Damon. A light, brighter than the sun at high noon, shone from the Messenger's golden-brown eyes, burning into the black eyes of the deceiver. Damon threw his hands up to shield his face, and the flesh on the back of his hands began to shrivel. "No!" he begged as he fell to his knees. The Messenger turned away from him and resumed his watch.

Damon struggled to his feet and stumbled down the steps to his bed in the galley. The following morning he rose from his bed and set out to find Brae. He laughed as the morning breeze ruffled his long black hair. Seeing Brae in the poop, taking his turn at the wheel, he called out in his boyish voice, "Hey, Brae! Let's grab some breakfast and then have some fun."

Brae grinned. Seeing Damon's bandaged hand, he asked, "Hey, what happened to you?"

Damon glanced at the Messenger standing at the wheel, his eyes fixed on the horizon, before answering, "Got hungry in the night. Tried to heat some soup but I guess I don't know how to work that old stove so well." He shrugged. "Don't worry, it's not as bad as it looks." Proud of his deception, he winked at the Messenger before taking off, with Brae right behind him, to scale the rigging.

Weeks passed with no sight of land. Brae thought they should at least have sighted an island by now. He wasn't yet very good at reading the maps, but he was working on it.

One afternoon, Brae went to the rail to stand beside the Messenger, whom he missed talking with. The Messenger seemed so distant, so aloof. *Maybe he is angry because I invited Damon on board without asking him first.* Brae took a deep breath. He knew he should talk to his old friend, but wasn't sure what to say.

"Is something wrong?" Brae asked.

"Yes," the Messenger answered quietly.

"Well?" Brae waited.

When the Messenger remained silent, Brae shrugged his shoulders and stomped away to find Damon. *What is troubling him?* Brae glanced back at the Messenger, standing with quiet dignity, like a soldier standing guard, and wondered again what the Messenger could see in the distance.

That evening, Damon asked Brae, "Whom should we shoot at dinner tonight?"

Expecting one of Damon's crude jokes, Brae laughed. "I don't know."

"The Messenger," Damon replied, laughing at his own humor.

Brae wasn't laughing. "Why would you say that?"

"Hey, I was just joking," Damon answered. "You know: 'Don't shoot the messenger...'"

But there was something in his eyes—something Brae had seen often somewhere before, probably in the City of Bondage. He couldn't figure out what it was, but it bothered him. Somehow, that *something* made hanging out with Damon a lot less fun.

One day, the Messenger told Brae to stay off the rigging.

"Why?" He and Damon asked in unison.

"Because there is a southeastern wind coming up and the rigging is not safe in high winds."

The Messenger went below and sat at a table in the galley, his eyes closed. He leaned on his elbows, his hands folded in front of him. For a long time he sat, head bowed in silence. A narrow shaft of sunlight streamed through the twelve-inch porthole to caress his silver-gray hair, cascading over his face and settling finally on his hands. They were strong hands, and used to work. His hands had navigated the *Seeking* through countless storms upon the Sea of Life, and had plucked many a sailor out of the debris of a ship wrecked upon submerged mountains. *With these hands I can rescue the perishing and repair broken ships,* he thought, *but never will I lift these hands to rescue or repair against the will of man.*

The silence was shattered by a terrified scream. The Messenger ran up the stairs, just in time to catch Brae as he tumbled from the top of the rigging. The Messenger stumbled under the impact, still holding Brae in his arms.

"Are you all right?" he asked, concern darkening his eyes.

Struggling to recover his breath, Brae pushed himself away from the Messenger and stood up. "Yeah," he puffed and walked off.

The Messenger followed Brae to his bunk. "What is the matter?" he asked.

"You jinxed that rigging, didn't you?" Brae accused. "Damon told me you would put a curse on the rigging so that I'd fall if I disobeyed you! That's what you did, isn't it? Well, isn't it?"

The Messenger stood up and left the room.

At dinner a couple of hours later, Damon did all the talking. Brae stared at his plate without eating. The Messenger ate in silence. Damon told one joke after another, and never seemed to notice that he was the only one laughing. As he passed the Messenger going up to the deck, he smirked at him behind Brae's back, a gesture the Messenger chose to ignore.

That night, Damon sat on Brae's bunk. "I still can't believe what the Messenger did to you." He bounced on the bed, slapping his hands against the covers with a jerky rhythm as if playing a drum. "That he would almost kill you just to prove he was right! You know, I'm thinking about leaving this old ship soon. Want to come with me in my purple raft? There's plenty of room for two."

Brae looked at Damon, surprised. Leave the ship? He had never thought of abandoning the journey. He said nothing, but he felt as if he had a rock in the pit of his stomach. He turned on his side and snuffed out his candle. Maybe he would feel better in the morning.

The following day, Damon was up early. "Hey, Brae!" He punched his arm. "Let's climb up into the crow's nest and see if we can spot some land."

The Messenger stood at the rail, looking toward the east. "No," he commanded. "You must not climb the rigging today."

When the Messenger went below, Damon made an obscene gesture at his back. Brae pretended not to notice. It was getting harder to overlook Damon's disrespect. Brae started to climb. But this time, even though Brae held his head as if looking up, he squinted down at Damon from the corner of his eye. He watched Damon go to the pole that held up the supporting beam beneath the crow's nest. He saw him slip out a bolt and then start on the next one. Damon was dismantling the beam so that the crow's nest would fall! By the time Brae was certain what Damon was doing, he was halfway to the crow's nest. Though he knew his words would be lost in the wind, Brae called out, "Help! Someone, help me!"

In a flash, the Messenger was on deck and had grabbed Damon. It appeared to Brae that a mighty wind had wrapped itself around the startled youth, lifted him over the rail, and deposited him, shrieking and cowering, onto the floor of the purple raft.

Brae came down from the crow's nest just in time to see Damon drift away. His hand was lifted—but Brae knew Damon well enough by now to know that he was not waving a fond farewell. Laughter, cruel and malevolent, emanated from the raft. Brae stared across the waves, terrified. The fiendish howls subsided as the raft drew near a huge shadow that rested upon the waves. The shadow lifted for a moment, and Brae realized that it hid a gigantic black ship.

Brae fell to his knees, bile rising in the back of his throat. The gigantic ship seemed alive with thousands of eyes that glowered at him through the thickening mist. Brae grasped the rail with trembling hands and pulled himself to his feet, choking as a dense sulfuric cloud rose from the black ship and dark shadows shot into the sky.

The Messenger stood at the rail beside Brae. "The dragon ship, *Avenger,*" he said, his eyes fixed on the ship. "The flagship of Dagog's fleet. It has been following us for weeks."

"The *Seeking* is like a toy next to that... thing." Brae said, his voice trembling.

The Messenger's hand tightened on the rail. "Dagog will not be pleased when the purple raft arrives without a captive."

"You knew who Damon was when he first came aboard our ship?"

"I know him," the Messenger said. "He may appear young, but he has been in the service of Dagog for ages. He has deceived many people, luring them into his raft and then delivering them into the hands of his master."

Brae, for once, was silent. "I am so stupid," he derided himself. He found that he now hated Damon as much as he had liked him before.

The Messenger frowned. "I remember another young man. His name was Alex. He, too, welcomed Damon aboard his ship. Alex was eighteen and thought himself wise. After a few months of Damon's company, Alex jumped into the purple raft with him and turned his back on the Other Kingdom."

The Messenger strode to the wheel and altered course, taking the *Seeking* far away from the *Avenger.*

Chapter Ten:

Umbler Rebuked

"That was not good." Lucacius wagged his shaggy head from side to side. "We give you a simple assignment and you are outsmarted by a *slave boy!*" Lucacius spit out the last words with distaste.

Umbler cringed, the dingy white feathers at the crown of his neck drooping. He sat, shoulders hunched, facing the wolven. A mist rose from his sweaty wings. Lucacius sniffed. The fragrance of fear always excited the wolven.

Lucacius licked his paw, allowing a bit of drool to trickle down his chin. "Do you wish to abdicate?"

"No!" Umbler was not ready to plead. "I have... an idea."

"Yeah?" Lucacius waited.

"Yeah," Umbler said, thinking fast. "A storm. We could stir up a storm."

The sound of Lucacius' laugh was not pleasant. "Do you really think you can do that?" he asked.

"Dagog—"

"Don't even think about it." Lucacius lay on the ground, his massive head resting on his paws, eyebrows tilted in disdain. "What do they teach these beasts in school these days?" he muttered under his breath.

"What?"

"Dagog cannot just whip up a storm like a child making bubbles in a bathtub." Lucacius' lips curled back in disgust.

"Then how—?" Umbler wished Lucacius would let him finish just one sentence.

"Dagog storms through the heavens, leaving a wake of wounded clouds behind. The warriors of the sky see the disturbance and war against our master. Sometimes the Emperor Himself comes down. He rides on the wings of the wind." Lucacius barely managed to conceal his glee. "Dagog has fallen from heaven more than once in the tempest of the Emperor's wrath. But if you ever speak of it..."

The words left unsaid dangled like Damocles' sword over Umbler's head.

"What do you suggest, most favored general?" he mumbled. Now he was ready to plead.

"You must not—I repeat must not—under any circumstances allow the subject to accept the Certificate of Redemption provided by Immon to those recruited by Mercy at the Cape of Conviction." Lucacius pointed toward a sandy shore rising out of the mists of the sea. "Do you see it yonder?"

Umbler nodded, unable to squeeze even the smallest sound through his constricted throat.

"You'd better think of something!" Lucacius tossed over his shoulder as he turned away from the junior dragon and sprinted off to find his master.

Umbler sat back on his tail, his eyes closed. Thinking with all his might.

CHAPTER ELEVEN:

The Trial

Several weeks later, at mid-morning, Brae began to feel a strange sense of foreboding. The sun grew dim and a dreary rain began to fall. He saw a murky shoreline through the mist that swirled across the restless waves.

"That," the Messenger said quietly, "is the Cape of Conviction."

As they drew closer, Brae could see the dingy gray buildings of a small town with an enormous masonry structure in the center of it. Squinting through the billowing mists, he saw that it had once been a prison, but the building was vacant now, its buttresses crumbling. The iron bars on the windows bled rusty stains down the sides of the formidable structure. Huge iron balls attached to thick chains lay strewn around a courtyard behind tall wrought-iron gates. A number of machines, apparently designed for torture, stood deteriorating in the front entry, worn with age and much use.

The sign above the portico had come loose on one side and now reclined at an angle against a ragged awning over the entryway. The word "CONDEMNED" was emblazoned in faded lettering against a once white background.

Brae wondered why the prison was abandoned. Had there been a rebellion that had overcome the prison guards and set the prisoners free?

He would rather go around this strange place, but something compelled him to anchor his ship and go ashore.

As soon as he set foot on land, Brae was surrounded by an angry mob. They swarmed from the ancient courthouse that rested on a solid rock beside the crumbling prison. The weathered stone building appeared strong, supported by the enormous rock on which it was built. The statue of a woman, crafted in bronze, graced the entrance to the massive building. With a somber frown, she scrutinized those who passed by, watching in grim silence as justice was carried out.

Someone grabbed Brae's shirt, ripping it from his back. Another reached out a strong, sinuous hand and locked steel cuffs around his wrists. A stooped old man took a rope from a bag that hung at this side and began wrapping it around Brae's ankles. He was half carried, half dragged before a tall, thin man dressed in black judicial robes. A wooden gavel rested on the bench before him.

"Fall to your knees in the presence of Justice!" a loud voice commanded.

Brae did so.

"Read the charges against this man," the loud voice said.

The judge picked up a thick scroll. As he unrolled it, Brae could see that it was very long and many things had been written on it. Brae was aghast. He had been a good man. How could he have broken the law? He trembled as he heard his crimes read aloud.

The judge began: "You, Brae—of the City of Bondage—are accused of living entirely for yourself without any regard to the harm you may have caused. You are accused of failing to do that which was good because you were unconcerned for the welfare of other people. In particular, you are accused..."

The list went on interminably. It included every unkind word Brae had ever spoken, every lie he had told, every cruel deed that had hurt someone, and every act of selfishness. Brae closed his eyes. *There is no hope for me,* he thought. *I am guilty!*

"Finally," the judge said, "you are accused of contributing to the death of the only blameless person to ever walk the earth in the Kingdom of Adawm. Your crime is punishable by death."

Falling on his face, Brae cried out for mercy! The crowd was silent as a man with a deeply lined face and snow-white hair approached the bench. He was twelve inches shorter than Brae but seemed much taller. His shoulders were straight, his eyes kind.

"I am Mercy," he said.

Brae's accusers bowed their heads. Without a word, Mercy took Brae by the hand and led him out of the building and along the streets to a place just outside the town.

Brae followed Mercy without protest, hesitating only when they reached the end of the dirt path and stopped before a vast, low-lying hill.

"This is the Hill of Death," Mercy said.

Rows and rows of white tombstones stood in solemn dignity against the gray clouds, monuments to those whose lives had passed. On the rounded peak of the Hill of Death, a mammoth silver birch tree raised its limbs to embrace the sky.

Mercy waved his hand toward the living monument. "This tree," he said, "is the place of execution and a monument to the one who died in your place."

"Why would anyone do that?" Brae was incredulous.

"The story is told in the Ancient Book of Mysteries," Mercy answered. "Have you not read it?"

Brae looked down. How could he tell Mercy that he had disdained the *Ancient Book*; that he had tried to ignore it though he knew it was intended to guide him on his way to the Other Kingdom.

Mercy looked into Brae's eyes with an intensity that frightened him. "Let us say that One who did no wrong had so great a heart that he could not enjoy the benefits of the Other Kingdom without giving everything he had in order to provide a second chance to those condemned to die. Does this interest you?"

"I don't understand it," Brae answered honestly.

"Well said." Mercy nodded his head with a vigor that startled Brae. "You will not understand until you accept the gift. You are still in Dagog's service."

"No. I will not serve Dagog."

"You believe that you have a choice?" Mercy thundered. His white hair, electrified by his passion, stuck out in all directions. His eyes, so kind just moments before, burned with the fire of his conviction. "You can serve the great King Addar or you can serve Dagog, but you must serve one or the other—because to fail to serve the one is to choose the other."

"I cannot choose." Brae's tortured voice betrayed the turmoil he experienced. He stood at the parting of ways and had no way of knowing the cost of choosing one over the other.

"The Wounded One offers you his life," Mercy said. "It is a free gift."

"How can this be?" Brae asked. "Where I come from, nothing is free."

"The gift is free, but it has been purchased for you at great cost," Mercy said.

"So it will cost me nothing?" Brae asked.

Mercy shook his head. "How can you not understand?" Then he answered his own question. "Your eyes are blinded to the truth, young Brae. Close your eyes."

Brae did so.

"What do you see?"

"I see a garden. It is as large as a city. It must be nearing harvest, for the produce is ripe."

"If I give you this field without exacting payment, is the field a free gift?"

"Yes!" Brae answered.

"Will it cost you anything?"

"No," Brae replied. "It is a gift."

"But if you accept this gift, you must cultivate the soil in the spring and then plant the seeds. You must weed the fields throughout the summer and stand guard over the tender fruit. It will be your responsibility to reap the harvest. And then you can enjoy the fruit of your labor. Does this cost you anything?"

"It costs me everything," Brae answered.

Mercy nodded.

Chapter Twelve:

Umbler Scores A Victory

"Do something!" Umbler squealed, wishing he had the courage to strike the grin from his commander's face. "You are supposed to help me!"

His fists were clenched at his side, his wings folded tightly against his belly. Rising up from the smoldering ashes of his defeat he took a step toward the wolven and tripped over a rotten log. His short legs flew upward, talons clutching at the wind, and he landed on his face in the muck. Squinting through the ooze, nostrils flared, he blew his breath out in great heaving gasps. "Dagog ordered you to instruct me." He seethed, embarrassment clouding his judgment.

The grin on the wolven's face was quickly replaced by a snarl and he whirled away from Umbler. "You'd better watch yourself," he growled.

Umbler stood his ground. "Well...?"

"Okay, here's how it is." Lucacius forgot his disdain for Umbler as he began to plot the demise of the subject. Coconspirators once again, the dragon and the wolven schemed away the night. For night it was in the domain of the Prince of the Darkness, though in the Kingdom of Adawm the sun peeked through mist and the clouds and time, it seemed, stood still.

CHAPTER THIRTEEN:

Beneath the Silver Birch Tree

Brae stared at the ancient silver birch tree that towered high above the Hill of Death. It cast its shade over all that lay beneath. Thousands of birds rested in its branches, their voices raised in harmonious song. Silvery heart-shaped leaves, the size of a man's hand, fluttered in the breeze, emitting a fragrance that was at once thrilling and soothing.

Brae wanted to embrace the tree, to throw his arms around its massive trunk and breathe deeply of its aroma. Somehow, he expected to find its trunk warm, responsive to his embrace.

But something deterred him—a premonition that if he did so, he would be forever changed, that the tree would become a part of himself, or he a part of the tree.

"Stop!" Brae looked around, hearing the command but seeing no one. The speaker once again intruded, as if from within his head. "You have been brought here to die! Run! Get away from this place as fast as you can!"

A flood of fear overwhelmed Brae, drowning him with doubt. Distrust, his old familiar companion, swept away the fragile longing that drew him to the tree. He took a step backward. "You are not ready to die." The voice was louder now, more confident. "You were a slave but now you are free.

A sudden determination seized Brae. "I will not give up my freedom." Suddenly, he hated this place! He jerked away from Mercy and began to run. He zigzagged between the tombstones and plunged into the surrounding forest, then circled around, heading for the beach.

The sun was setting over the emerald waters of the Sea of Life when Brae climbed into his rowboat and returned to the *Seeking*. He glanced over his shoulder, amazed that he could still see the silver birch tree that stood upon the hill, enveloped in the crimson light of the setting sun.

Far away in the Other Kingdom, Emperor Addar and his son, King Immon, known to many as the Wounded One, sat upon their thrones, watching as Brae fled the Cape of Conviction. In his hand, Immon held a parchment that bore the words "Brae, former slave of Meriquoi." At the top was the heading "Certificate of Redemption."

Addar patted his son's hand. "You are disappointed."

"The young believe time belongs to them." Immon shook his head.

"Dagog knows better. The trap has been set."

Umbler danced upon the clouds. "Yeah, yeah, yeah," he exulted. "I did it. I'm the best." Fantasies of reveling in his master's pleasure had his head spinning until he bumped into Lucacius just as he was coming out of a billowing black thunderhead. Umbler blinked, unprepared for the hard smack the irritated wolven delivered to his grinning face.

"What did you do that for?" he asked, rubbing his chin, careful not to disturb the wart that dangled from his cheek. Every time it wiggled, Lucacius mocked him, and Umbler had experienced enough ridicule from his commander. He would not allow Lucacius to steal his thunder—not this time.

"You fool," Lucacius growled, and Umbler began to suspect that the wolven's anger had nothing to do with getting bumped. His glee melted like salt in the rain.

"What?" Umbler tried unsuccessfully to keep the tremor from his voice.

"Dagog is about to strike you from the force." Lucacius seemed pleased to deliver the news.

"Why? I don't—"

"Shut up, you fool!"

Umbler closed his mouth so quickly that he severed the tip of his tongue. He didn't dare open his mouth to spit. Lucacius looked ready to explode, his eyes wild, his hackles raised. Umbler tasted blood. He swallowed hard, gagging on the bitterness of his disappointment.

Head sagging between his shoulders, Umbler waited. Lucacius

seemed in no hurry to speak.

"You let him see the tree." The wolven seethed. "You let him hear the Truth. Do you think this is a victory?"

"He listened to me," Umbler said. "Why do you think—"

"That he didn't bend the knee?" Lucacius finished. "Because he still thinks as a slave. Because the City of Bondage resides within him still. And possibly, because of your words in his head. But your words were inadequate. He has seen the tree, felt its power. Do you think he will forget? You are a fool."

Umbler's head sank lower into his hunched shoulders, and blood drizzled from the corners of his mouth. He raked his hand across his face, accidentally setting off the inflamed wart, which swung first left and then right.

Lucacius fixed his eyes upon the wart, distracted, irritated by the movement. A movement he could not control... unless... In one quick move, he leapt at the face of the despairing dragon, clamped his teeth upon the offending wart, and bit down—hard.

"Eeeeeeeeeeee!" Umbler's squeal echoed through the corridors of Darkness. The wart may have been ugly and a nuisance at times, but in the world of Darkness it was a sign of his stature. He had been robbed. Howling, the dragon fell on his face.

After a time he sat up, swiped the blood from his cheek, and resolved that Brae, former slave of Meriquoi, his first "subject" in the Kingdom of Adawm, would pay for this. Suddenly, his suffering had purpose. Umbler, junior dragon in the service of Dagog, felt his wings stiffen and he raised them high, catching a swift current as it swept past. He had work to do.

Bill of Rights and Ancient Creed of the Land of Lasciviousness

In this Land
Lasciviousness
Is the Order of the Day
No one forces others
To do as One may say.
But all are free to dress—or not
To come and go at will
To be the person that will please
Himself and no one else.
Lasciviousness you may have heard
Is evil—Poppycock!
Superstitions such as this
Are not for the evolved.

By our Law:

All should live uncensored
By a public-minded view
Whatever is right in your own eyes
Is the righteous thing to do.

CHAPTER FOURTEEN:

Land of Lasciviousness

The Messenger was quiet when Brae returned from the Cape of Conviction. He seemed disappointed. "What did he expect me to do?" Brae fumed. He felt irritable, and avoided the Messenger whenever he could.

Late one evening, Brae sighted land. He was tired of sailing, and couldn't wait to get his feet on the ground. He tugged at the ropes securing the rowboat. *Why can't I get it loose?* he thought, frowning in irritation.

The Messenger came to stand beside him. "Where are you going?"

"Obviously, I am going ashore," Brae muttered.

"There is danger on this island," the Messenger warned. "It is called the Land of Lasciviousness—"

"I don't see anything wrong with it," Brae interrupted, refusing to look toward the shoreline, vaguely visible through the thick mist. Shrill laughter pierced the haze, and music—loud and chaotic—boomed across the water, echoing against the sides of the *Seeking.*

Ignoring the concerned gaze of the Messenger, Brae turned abruptly, launched the boat, and rowed hard toward the island.

Invisible fingers covered his ears so that he could not hear the monster's laughter as it glided behind the clouds, hidden from the boy so eagerly rowing toward disaster. Umbler roared his pleasure.

Pulling his boat ashore, Brae watched the natives dance wildly around a huge bonfire, their naked bodies glistening with perspiration and perfumed oil, strong and sweet.

By the time he approached the fire, Brae's feet were moving with the music. Soon he was leaping and shouting along with the natives as they worshipped the fire and paid homage to the god of the night.

Intent upon the dancers that surrounded him, Brae did not see that the Messenger followed him ashore and now watched him from the shadows. The wise eyes of the Messenger looked beyond the flailing arms and legs of the dancers and the faces of the leering men who sat beside the fire. Looking deeper, he could see the disease rotting away a young man's heart as he laughed and lusted after forbidden fare.

Unheeded, the Messenger turned away to walk among the inhabitants of the Land of Lasciviousness. Even here, in this wicked land, the light would shine in the morning.

CHAPTER FIFTEEN:

A Gift Bestowed

The Messenger stood before the Imperial Emperor Addar.

"You have come from the Land of Lasciviousness," the emperor said.

The Messenger nodded.

Addar stood before his throne. "Immon has spoken for our child who stumbles in the darkness."

"Brae has been deceived by Umbler, servant of Dagog. He stumbles but he will soon recover," the Messenger predicted. "I have sent Suffering to visit him. Suffering is the greatest of our teachers."

"And what of the Land of Lasciviousness? What have you seen there?"

"Everywhere I went throughout that land, I saw enslaved people, bound with great chains to Dagog. Everywhere they go they drag their chains with them. It makes them incredibly weary, but they do not understand why. They do not even seem to be aware that they are in chains.

"This seemed strange to me. Why could they not feel the weight of the iron, the chafing of their flesh? How could they ignore the bruising tugs against their limbs by the monster that enslaves them? And then I realized that they all draw their water from a stagnant pool in the center of the land, a foul-smelling swamp the inhabitants of the land call 'Dagog's well.' I discerned that this numbs and seduces them so that they cannot see what is right in front of them."

"They are intoxicated by pleasure, terrified by the truth," said the emperor. "It is time." Immon rose from his throne and crossed the room. He opened the door to an adjoining room, allowing a stream of amber light to flood the white light of the throne room. He stepped inside. Around the walls, golden brackets attached shelves of mother of pearl. The shelves held vases of exquisite pottery and crystal vials, some overlaid with precious metals, and others adorned with rubies, sapphires, and diamonds. But the outward beauty of the vessels was meager compared to the value of their contents.

Immon selected a small crystal vial and returned to his throne, closing the door behind him. The Messenger stood, waiting.

Will I never cease to tremble when Immon places the vial in my hand? he thought, staring at the object—about three inches long and half an inch in diameter—that lay in the center of his trembling palm.

The vial felt warm and radiated a soft golden light, like the light that shone from the silver birch tree embossed on the cover of the *Ancient Book of Mysteries.*

"Go now!" Immon resumed his throne. "The time is short."

The Messenger, holding the vial firmly in his hand, nodded and stepped backwards.

In the days that followed, the Messenger visited every dwelling in the Land of Lasciviousness, even those hidden deep in the forest. Those who welcomed him would never be the same, for the Messenger spoke to them the words of the *Ancient Book of Mysteries,* and the life that flowed through the words like a living light warmed their hearts. He reached out his hand and touched their eyes and something like blinders fell from them. They now saw the monster that they had been chained to for so many years, and wondered that they were alive. The wild eyes and frenzied fury of the beast sent spasms of terror through their hearts. They gagged at the white flecks of foam that clung to his sooty cheeks, choked on the stench of his breath. They struggled to free themselves from the chains that bound them to the monster, but found the effort futile. When their strength was spent, then they were ready.

They came to the Messenger as moths to the light. Fragile, helpless, and afraid they came, no longer frightened by death, but terrified by the beast that consumed them. They trembled as the Messenger said, "This is the oil of the silver birch tree, which stands on a hill in the Cape of Conviction. The tree is a monument to the One who died there with terrible suffering. By his blood he paid the price, and by his life he offers pardon to all who acknowledge their need of it. It is reserved for those who have been tried and found guilty of treason, as you have, one and all. By the touch of this oil, you will enter into his suffering, and through the passage of his suffering you will be pardoned. If this is your desire, then bend your knee and receive the free gift that was provided for you at unspeakable cost to Immon, your king and rightful ruler over this land.

As they did so, their heavy chains fell off, like dried leaves before a powerful wind. Like children born anew from the womb of death, they laughed and danced, hugged each other and cried.

There was one among them who felt their joy and rejoiced with them, but his joy was tempered by knowledge of the suffering that awaited the servants of Immon in the Land of Lasciviousness. He would be there—in the midst of it he would feel their pain, experience their sorrow. But he would not intervene, for that is the way of the Kingdom. The Fellowship of Suffering, while excruciating to those who enter into it, is the pathway to intimacy with the Wounded One, who suffered more than any other who ever came before or who will come after him in the Kingdom of Adawm. And those who enter The Fellowship of His suffering will find that for each cup of pain suffered in his service, there is an ocean of joy stored up for the sufferer in the Other Kingdom.

CHAPTER SIXTEEN:

Sadie

She was bent and wrinkled, and even in youth she had attracted few admirers. She had resigned herself long ago to a solitary life and lived alone in a miserable hovel at the edge of the land. Sadie had no stomach for the feasts of pleasure or the rituals of fire that consumed most of the residents of the Land. She gained her small self-respect in the only way she could—by becoming a seer. And for this she was well known and sometimes feared.

She had watched the young man, Brae from the shadows since the day he stepped foot on the shores of the land. She despised his deceptive charm, which soon dissipated among the inhabitants of the Land as she had known it would, but there was still something about him—some seeking, some vulnerability—that touched a tender spot in her otherwise hardened heart.

I cannot learn his secret by listening to the boy, she thought. *He is consumed already by the Land and is not himself. I will follow the one who came in his shadow.* For she had noticed that the Messenger appeared immediately after Brae, and she alone had noted that no boat or raft had born him to shore. Sadie had seen a white dove, as large almost as an eagle, alight—not in the trees but in the shadow of the trees. She believed, though she would dare tell no one, that the Messenger was indeed one and the same as the beautiful dove.

Once, he caught her staring at him. She quickly looked away, expecting rejection or ridicule. In that brief glance she knew that this Messenger was no ordinary man. For the first time in her seventy-eight years Sadie experienced love. The eyes that met hers were like no other. Something long frozen in Sadie's heart began to thaw, just a little, around the edges. Emotions that had been denied her flooded over her, and she turned away and shuffled back to her hovel as quickly as her arthritic feet could carry her. There, she sat before her fire, took out a wooden pipe and filled it with the dried grass, and puffed away until long after the stars and the moon had circuited the sky. And then, she had gone in search of the Messenger.

And now, here she was, rising from a bended knee to stand before him. The old seer stood silently. Words, her only trade, forsook her now. He reached out his hand and wrapped an arm around Sadie. "My daughter," he said. "Do you understand what has happened to you today?"

Sadie nodded. Then, as if a well of water gushed from the depths of her being, bringing life to the dormant seeds of joy and hope, truth and patience, and finally peace, Sadie burst into song:

She who had no purpose
Who wandered all alone
Has been found of the king
Who sits on His throne.
For seventy-eight years
I have wandered in fear
In darkness and hatred
And never a tear.
The life I have wasted
Is given anew
Immon, my great king
I give my life to you.

A little girl began to clap her hands. She stood beside her parents, who also clapped. Then others joined in and shouts of joy began to rise from the lips of all. Men, women, and children encircled the old woman. Some touched her shoulder, her arm, while others hugged her, their tears mingling with hers.

When they all stepped back, Sadie stood in the center of a circle of friends. "Oh!" the little girl said, "Sadie, you are so beautiful."

And indeed she was. Her skin, though wrinkled, glowed softly, as if touched by the sun. Her eyes sparkled, and the color, blue as the waters of the deep, was so intense that one could almost fall into it; and Sadie's smile transformed her plain face into a cameo of goodness.

The following day, the little girl, whose name was Salina, came to visit Sadie, and was once again amazed. For the miserable hovel where the old woman had lived for so long had been transformed. The floors were swept clean and the dishes washed and put away. A sweet fragrance, like the oil of the silver birch tee, permeated the house. Sadie welcomed the girl, who thereafter came often to talk with her and enjoy her company.

CHAPTER SEVENTEEN:

Chief Sodomon

Those who had been freed from their chains met every night in a clearing deep in the forest far from the city. Others who knew of their clandestine meetings were both envious and angry. They sensed their freedom and wanted to have it, but did not want to give up their pleasures. They called those who followed the Messenger "Resisters." The name seemed to fit.

Their leader was an old man who had suffered long in the Land of Lasciviousness. He was a rebel from the start. At the age of six, Surice was punished for refusing to dance to the fire god. At twelve he was beaten for refusing to follow the rites of manhood, which demanded that he join his fellows in a ritual of such lewdness that it would not be proper to describe it.

Surice was happier than most citizens, for he made his home in the jungle and rarely came into the city. A crystal stream that flowed past his humble hut offered pure, sweet water, and he married and raised his family in the peace of the deep woods.

When the Messenger came to the land, Surice was the first to respond to his invitation. A Resister already, he welcomed both the Messenger and his message.

Late at night, while the forest was still draped in darkness, over a hundred Resisters huddled close around a forbidden fire, seeking warmth and comfort—warmth because the night was chilly, comfort, because death, like the shadow of a great raptor, hovered over them. "One day," Surice said, "death will swoop down upon us, and we will be transported to live forever in the Other Kingdom."

The Resisters were lawbreakers, every one of them. It had been decreed in ages past that all citizens in the Land of Lasciviousness must prove their allegiance to the Prince of the Darkness by the ritual dance. It was required that they shed their clothes and dance before the fire to the god of the night.

The Resisters, who pledged their allegiance to Immon, refused to dance—refused to pay homage to the Prince of the Darkness.

Chief Sodomon, ruler of the Land of Lasciviousness, sat in his tent deep in conversation with one who visited often at the fire of the Resisters.

"They believe," the spy reported, "that a great king, Immon, is at war with one called Dagog, who rules over the Kingdom of Adawm, including the Land of Lasciviousness. They say this ruler is evil and they oppose him. They believe that you are under the rule of Dagog."

"Therefore, they oppose me!" Sodomon turned pale. Few had dared challenge his authority. He was furious. Wrapping his robe closer to his body, he stood, pacing before the fire that burned in the center of his dwelling, casting strange shadows on the walls. The forms of wolvens, whelter, and other ancient mystics crept and floated along the stained leather walls as the flames flickered.

"Evil!" Sodomon spat the word from his mouth. "A superstition. Those who speak of evil speak only to condemn others."

After a moment's silence, Sodomon continued. "By refusing to dance before the fire, these Resisters condemn those who do."

"Onidah!" The spy hissed through a toothless smirk. "They commit onidah." Already he could taste blood. He began to quote the ancient creed:

All should live uncensored

By a public-minded view

Whatever is right in your own eyes

Is the righteous thing to do.

"Harmony in the Land of Lasciviousness depends upon the inherent right of every person to do what is right in his own sight without censure or condemnation," the spy whined.

His contorted face appeared insanely ugly to Sodomon as the spy quoted the remedy of the law: "He who censures the actions of another is guilty of onidah, and he who is guilty of onidah shall be put to death." His thick lips twisted, and he licked them repeatedly, like a lizard about to feast.

"And death it shall be." Sodomon stopped his pacing and turned toward the shadowy forms that loitered against the wall like ethereal witnesses. "I will strip them of their clothes and force them to dance. And if they refuse to dance, they will die."

Sodomon's face felt hot, and the heat in his hut seemed oppressive. He stepped outside, relishing the cool breeze sweeping through the palms. He plopped down in the lush grass front of his shelter, feeling quite pleased with himself. He looked up—into the face of the Messenger. Fear gripped his heart. Those eyes—they seemed to penetrate the flesh and see into his soul. As if looking into a mirror, Sodomon trembled as he stared into the boiling caldron of lust, hatred, filth, and disease that consumed him. Then, like a broken mirror, the image shattered. Chief Sodomon stood up and spit on the ground at the Messenger's feet. He turned away and promptly forgot what manner of man he was.

The Messenger resumed walking and was soon obscured by the foliage at the edge of the forest. "I know where you are going," Sodomon fumed, "you and your... Resisters, hiding like vermin in the night!"

Watching the bushes close behind the Messenger, Sodomon realized that he hated him—hated him more than the rival chief who had killed his brother, more than the woman who had deserted him after a year of marriage. All of his hatred suddenly had focus. This man—this Messenger—was an enemy above all others. Sodomon wanted to kill him, flay him alive before the entire village, to make an example of him.

But he knew that he wouldn't. He feared him too much to lay a hand on him.

CHAPTER EIGHTEEN:

A Conference in the Other Kingdom

The Imperial Emperor Addar was seated on his throne. King Immon sat beside him, gazing into the distance. His jaw tightened. The old scars on his back tingled, reminding him of his suffering in the Kingdom of Adawm.

Addar looked into the Land of Lasciviousness, his eyes blazing with anger. Standing, he raised his hand against the land. Chief Sodomon, pacing before his fire plotting the death of innocent men, women, and children, stood on the brink of destruction. Molten fire, like lava, began bubbling up from the depths of the earth beneath his feet. The land trembled. The ground beneath Chief Sodomon's feet grew warm, then hot. A crevice began to open.

"No!" Immon stood to face his Father, his hand on Addar's shoulder. Indicating the Certificate of Redemption he held in his hand, he insisted, "He is mine, Father. Look." He motioned to a translucent being standing like a soldier at attention, his golden hair brushing his broad shoulders. "Andrae, start the scene."

Addar watched the replay of Chief Sodomon's life. There he was—a little boy, maybe five years old. He was crying, running the gauntlet. Older warriors with ugly symbols drawn on their faces mocked the child. "Cry, little baby girl!" they shouted. "Cry, baby!" Stones were hurled, bruising the young boy. His tears turned to anger, and by the time he reached the end of the gauntlet, he seized an old hag by the hair and threw her to the ground. "Mother," he hissed. "You should not have taught me to be weak. You should have taught me not to cry."

"A little more time," Addar agreed.

The King sat down. Immon took his place beside him.

"Tomorrow," Addar said, "the Messenger sails for other lands."

"He has won many followers in the Land of Lasciviousness." Immon counted those huddled around the fire. "One hundred twenty-four."

"They will not be discouraged," Addar predicted. "The Messenger has touched their eyes."

"So that they see beyond the veil." Immon completed Addar's thought, as he often did. "Just like our followers in ancient times who were thrown to the lions, torched, and mutilated—but whose spirits escaped the edge of the sword, escaped unscathed into the Other Kingdom."

Addar settled back on his throne. Immon closed his eyes, imparting strength to those who lived under threat of death in the Land of Lasciviousness.

CHAPTER NINETEEN:

A Sad Farewell

The Messenger stood with his back to the fire, his head bowed. His followers rose and ran to him, embraced him. A little girl with black braids that hung to her waist clung to him, sobbing.

The Messenger lifted her in his arms. "Salina," he whispered. "Do not fear. I will never forsake you."

Salina cried, "But you said we won't see you at our fires. You are going away!"

"Salina," the Messenger asked, "do you see the wind?"

The child shook her head. Her enormous eyes fixed on the Messenger's with an intensity that is uncomfortable to everyone except small children.

"Do you see the love that fills your heart?"

Again, the child shook her head. "No."

"But you know that it is there. Even so, know that I am with you always."

Handing the child to her father, the Messenger turned from them and disappeared into the forest. There he knelt beside a mossy stone and sobbed, his shoulders heaving, tears falling like drops of rain onto the stone. He agonized over the suffering that the Resisters would soon endure. He willed them to be strong.

He stood up and turned toward the village. Dry leaves crumbled beneath his feet, and twigs snapped from the trees as he pushed his way through the forest. Things had changed in the Land of Lasciviousness. A drought had settled in, turning the forests brown and the crops to dust. The once prosperous land had become gaunt and cadaverous.

Standing in the shadows, the Messenger could see the great fire in the heart of the village and the figures dancing around it. And there among them was the one who had forsaken his journey. "Why would this young man, once freed from the tyranny of Meriquoi, choose to live like this?" The Messenger grieved. He watched as a figure in a gray robe emerged from the darkness. He stood over seven feet tall. A pointed hood covered his head and most of his face. The Messenger looked grim. He knew this stranger. It was Suffering. Even in a crowd, he was hard to miss, yet Suffering sought no recognition. Only those who have been introduced know him. And those who have never forget.

Brae danced beside the fire with his usual companions. His sightless eyes did not see the hooded figure approaching him. Like a supple weeping willow branch, Suffering bent from the waist and whispered something in Brae's ear. He continued dancing as if he hadn't heard, so Suffering tapped him on the shoulder. Startled, Brae jumped to the right, knocking Surgie, nephew of Sodomon, to the ground. Surgie grabbed a handful of small stones and hurled them in Brae's direction. Someone else grabbed a club and took a swing at Surgie. He missed, and the club hit the person standing next to Surgie. A look of amazement spread over the poor man's face just before he went down. Blood spurted from a gash on his head.

Brae moved away from the fire, melting into the shadows. Too late. An enraged man, welding a wooden club, turned on Brae. "You are the cause of all this trouble," he said. "You bring bad luck. We should never have let you dance at our fire."

"Yes!" others agreed.

Chief Sodomon appeared, his wrath fueled by the wilted crops in the fields and the assault on his nephew. "Bind him!" he ordered. "Throw him into the stone house. We will burn him in the fire tomorrow night. Then, perhaps, when his body lies in ashes, the rains will come...."

Chapter Twenty:

A Second Chance for Umbler

There was a party in the middle clouds—that place of Darkness where Dagog rules. The master himself, having returned from one of his many journeys, occupied a towering column of sodden clouds. His forces gathered around him like a flock of vultures hungry for plunder.

Stretching out his arm, Dagog extended a soot-blackened hand toward his forces. All fell down and worshipped him. "Arise, my friends," his gravelly voice rose above the murmur. "This is no day to bow—for today we celebrate. Release our brother."

Lucacius nodded at one who stood nearby, and a hunchbacked wist turned toward the dragon, who cowered in his chains. The stench of death met the worshippers' nostrils as Umbler rose to his feet and stumbled toward his master. There was a sigh of relief among the worshippers as the junior dragon stood. The horde of hellish monsters were relieved to see one among them given a second chance, because not one of them was sure of his own success. Every assignment had its possibilities.

Umbler fell on his face at Dagog's feet, wondering at his release. Dagog reached out his hand and Umbler forgot his broken wings, forgot that his teeth were crushed by the master in his rage when the Resisters began to rebel against their chains. "Of course," Umbler conceded, "it was my fault. If I had not failed my assignment, the *Seeking* may have passed the shores of the Land of Lasciviousness."

"Tomorrow," Dagog announced, "the boy dies. Though Umbler was incompetent, we should celebrate our victory... and the boy was his assignment. What do you say?"

The crowd roared its agreement. Always, they agreed with Dagog. And always they were in favor of a feast.

"Tomorrow at sunrise, when the ashes of the deserter rise on the wind—then we celebrate!"

Those who dwell in the Kingdom of Adawm pulled their covers over their ears and complained about the storm that split the heavens. Never were the winds more fierce, the lightning more ferocious than on that night. Umbler shuffled through the corridors of Darkness with glazed eyes and broken wings, dreading the sunrise. He had a strange and awful premonition that celebration was premature.

Chapter Twenty-one:

A Prisoner Set Free

As he lay on the cold stone floor, tears flowed down Brae's battered face and fell on his trembling hands. Regret visited him in his cold cell, sitting quietly beside him. Brae put his hands over his face and closed his eyes.

"This is the life you chose when you ran away from the Hill of Death at the Cape of Conviction," Regret said in a trembling voice.

"I am a liar and a cheat," Brae said. "I deserve to die."

Regret nodded. "You had your chance. You sailed away from the City of Bondage—a free man."

Brae looked at the messenger of Truth who sat beside him, his hand resting on Brae's arm. Regret was not an unfriendly sort, but rather comforting. In his present circumstance Regret seemed to be his only friend, perhaps his only hope as well.

As if reading his thoughts, Regret said, "I cannot release you from this prison. Your choices have brought you here, and they alone can help you now."

My choices, Brae thought. *I cannot undo that which I have already done. I can look back, as Regret has forced me to do, but to go back is impossible.*

"As long as there is life, Brae," Regret said, "Choice will be your companion; and every Choice you accept will bring with him other Choices yet to be accepted or rejected."

As the full moon sailed over the tops of the ancient mamboni trees and a cold wind blew through the bars of his cell, Brae curled into a ball and hugged his chest. How he longed to return to the silver birch tree at the Hill of Death, to sit beneath its shade and wrap his arms around its massive trunk. He could almost smell the fragrance of the silvery-green leaves; hear the voices of a thousand birds singing in harmony from its branches.

I am going to die, he thought, b*ut I am not going to depart the Kingdom of Adawm without offering an apology to the one who rescued me from the City of Bondage.*

Kneeling on the cold stone floor, Brae began. "I do not know, O Great King, if my words will be heard, but I must speak them. I'm so sorry, Immon. I know that you did your best to rescue me from the death that never ends—but I was unwilling to enter the fellowship of your suffering. The judge was right. I am guilty. I cared nothing for that which cost you so much."

A strong wind rattled the iron bars on the small window just above Brae's head and the sound of wings swept the sky, drawing ever nearer the boy who hugged his arms across his chest, waiting for the inevitable.

When nothing happened, the stillness became unbearable. He looked up into the small patch of sky above his head. He gasped at the sight of a large white dove perched on the window ledge, pressed against the iron bars. "I will never leave you or forsake you." Though unspoken, the words were clear.

Brae closed his eyes and breathed deeply of the sweet fragrance that blew through the room. The scent of the silver birch tree permeated the room and carried with it peace like a river. Unstoppable, incomprehensible, incomparable peace. Brae gasped as he was swept away, carried back to a place at the foot of the silver birch tree. He knew that his body did not move, it was compelled by bars and chains to remain in a cell, but he suddenly understood how Belita could say that she was free while she served as a slave to Meriquoi. The body is dust and ashes, Brae thought. And the spirit that bows before the great King Immon cannot be enslaved.

Brae knelt at the foot of the enormous birch tree and pledged his allegiance to the King of all Kings who had died to purchase the Certificate of Redemption for a rebellious slave boy in the City of Bondage.

If I die, Brae thought, *at least I will die free!*

Those who lingered outside the stone building, keeping watch over the one who would be burned in the fire tomorrow, soon found themselves in a deep sleep.

As the pale blush of morning crept across the gray stone floor, Brae heard a noise above his head and looked up—into the face of the Messenger. He reached up a hand, and the Messenger grasped it. He pulled Brae up, right out of his chains and his prison cell into the early morning light.

Brae took the Messenger's arm, walking with him between the huts of sleeping villagers. The Messenger helped him into the rowboat. Moments later, they stood on the deck of the good ship *Seeking*.

Brae stood in awkward silence, staring at the deck, reluctant to turn away but at a loss for words.

"Go to bed, Brae," the Messenger said, not unkindly. "Sleep. You will need your strength tomorrow."

Brae slept, and dreamed of Belita. Meriquoi stood over her with his whip raised. His muscles rippled beneath a thin shirt; his face twisted in rage. Most masters handed the whip to a strong slave, one trained in exacting pain without injuring the master's property. Damaged slaves lost their value. But Meriquoi preferred to administer punishment personally. He could well afford to replace dead or injured slaves with new arrivals from the slavers. Meriquoi grinned, his crooked teeth gleaming in the moonlight. Brae screamed when the whip descended on the naked back of the helpless woman. "No!" Still sleeping, he rolled off his bed onto the floor, striking his head against a post. Why can't I wake up? The whip rose and fell with sickening thuds. Belita remained motionless, silent. Blood seeped from a gash on Brae's head and mingled with the blood that flowed down Belita's back.

Brae felt himself drifting, floating on a river of tears. The sun was shining, but it was not hot, because a cool breeze stirred the waves. "The current—where is it taking me?"

Belita! She was standing on a shore of golden sand, her wounds healed. She was walking, running. She stepped into the river and glided swiftly toward the other side. Swathed in white drapery, she glowed like the light, like the sun. Brae shaded his eyes. Reaching the far shore, she turned toward him, her beautiful brown eyes smiling at him. Her face was radiant. Lifting a hand, she waved goodbye. Suddenly, she was surrounded by a host of others, shining like herself, all dressed in white. She reached out and they took her hands.

One stood out from the rest, blinding in his radiance. Belita cried out, "My king!"

The brightness overcame Brae, and he saw no more.

The pastel curtain of dawn draped itself across the sky before Brae's eyes opened. He pulled himself up to sit on his narrow bunk, holding his aching head in trembling hands. With a sense of awe, Brae realized that while he slept, the veil had parted, giving him a glimpse into the Other Kingdom.

Brae knew that Belita had died because of him, and for many years he had carried the bitter weight of that guilt. Now it was as if that oppressive burden had dissolved in a river of tears. He had an overwhelming sense that he was forgiven. Belita, at last, was free, and that meant that Brae too was free—free to live, free to remember.

So many years ago, a lifetime ago, in the City of Bondage, Belita had taught Brae to believe in the existence of the Other Kingdom, filled his young heart with hope of freedom. But Brae could not comprehend freedom as Belita knew it, for Belita believed that it was possible to be free even in the City of Bondage. "When you know the truth," she used to say, "then you are free."

"How can I be free while Meriquoi is my master?" The words were bitter in Brae's mouth.

"Real freedom lies within," Belita said. "No one can take that kind of freedom from you."

Brae was disgusted. He wanted to be free in his body as well as his mind. Anything less was not freedom, but deception. He dreamed of escape. He planned for it. And finally he tried to achieve it. But the captain of the guard caught him, pinned him to the ground, and ground his booted foot into Brae's back, waiting for Meriquoi to come and mete out punishment to his prisoner.

He did not have to wait long. Meriquoi arrived within minutes, flushed with anger. A powerful man, he could have killed a slave with his bare hands, but he preferred the whip. It inflicted greater pain. Cursing, Meriquoi straddled Brae's back.

But the whip never lashed the back of the terrified youth, for Belita launched herself across the cobbled road and covered Brae with her own body. "One life for another!" she implored. "This youth will bring you much gain on the slave block, Master, while I, a woman past my prime, am nearly useless to you. It is not his fault that he has done this, for I am the one who fueled his desire for freedom. I encouraged him."

Meriquoi hesitated. "Get up, dog!" he commanded.

Belita did not move.

The whip descended in fury. It stripped the cloth from Belita's back in one stroke and found the flesh beneath.

Brae was paralyzed by fear. This could not be happening. He couldn't speak, couldn't move. Between lashes, Belita whispered against his ear, "The greatest love in the world is this—" The whip cut into her back. Brae could feel the impact through her body. He cringed. "—to give up your life for a friend." Another lash. A ragged breath. "You are my friend, Brae." Her voice grew faint, so that he had to strain to hear. "When you know the truth—" An awful gasp, like air escaping from a bellows. Then faintly "—the truth will make you free." The breathing stopped.

Meriquoi tossed the whip to the guard and stomped away. The guard spat, "Dog!" Then he too turned and walked away, leaving Brae lying on the street, Belita clinging to his back even in death.

Brae stumbled to his feet. Gathering the broken body into his arms, he carried Belita outside the city gates and buried her. Stacking stones over the freshly turned dirt, he wrote a memorial for the only person who had ever loved him: "HERE LIES BELITA. SHE DIED FREE."

A week later, the Messenger had come to the City of Bondage to rescue one who had been waiting for him.

His tears spent, Brae curled up on the bunk and slept. Peace coursed through his battered soul like a life-giving river; forgiveness freely given was at last received.

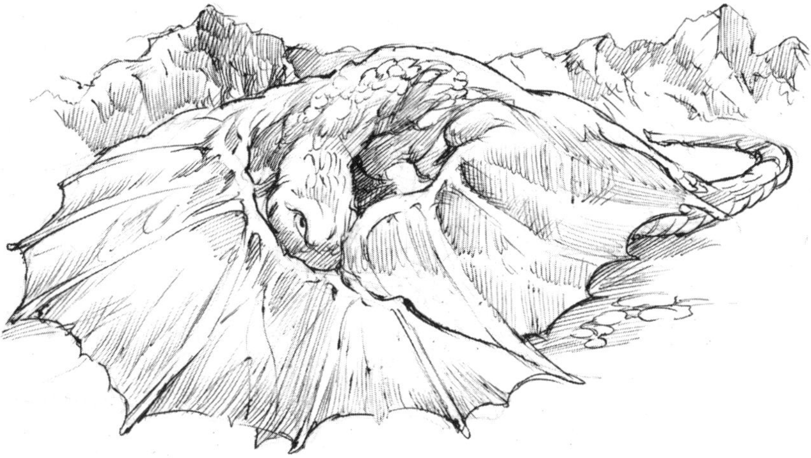

CHAPTER TWENTY-TWO:

The End of Umbler

Umbler saw the master coming. There was no place to hide. No escape. He fell on the ground, covering his face with a broken wing. The thunder of heavy steps drew near. Umbler could not breathe. He peeked out from beneath the wing and fainted dead away. Dagog, followed by Lucacius, advanced with murder in his eyes. There would be no second chances. *I should have known* was the last thought Umbler remembered.

And it would have been his last thought ever, except for his unbelievable luck. At the last moment, as someone told him later, a spear of lightning zapped through the sky, white-hot flame searing the heavens, singeing hide and fur alike. *So the scream I heard was not my own,*

Umbler thought, *but Dagog's as he fell, once again, from his throne.* If a dragon could smile, and mean it, Umbler might have done so, but he was already scheming his way back into his master's goodwill.

I have a little time, he thought, *Dagog will not be throwing his kicks around until his own bottom recovers.* If a dragon could be thankful, Umbler would have been thankful to whomever it may have been that was big enough to kick his master's butt."

CHAPTER TWENTY-THREE:

Crashed on the Rocks

Early one morning, the Messenger told Brae to turn the ship out of the open sea and follow a strange and unfamiliar course. He turned the ship into a narrow channel between the cliffs of the mainland and a series of rocky islands. Brae laughed as he watched the wind fill the sails. The years had put lines on his face and hair on his chin, but had failed to dull his excitement about his journey. He could hardly wait to explore the new lands they were approaching.

Above the sound of the waves that slapped against the sides of the ship, Brae heard what sounded like a feeble cry for help. With the cry came another sound that brought fear to his heart, a distant roar that grew louder each moment as the wind drove the *Seeking* farther along the channel. The tide was roaring through the ever-narrowing waterway, churning into whirlpools and smashing against the cliffs on both sides. A milky mist rose from the giant cascade of water.

Silently, Brae turned to the Messenger. Had the time come for him to die? He was willing to accept his fate with courage and dignity.

"We must go on, Brae, not to die, but to bring life. There is a sound louder than the wind and stronger than the water. Listen with your heart, and you will know why you have been drawn to this place."

Peering into the billowing mist, Brae could see a vision of faces—sad faces of men, women, and children who were lost and struggling to stay afloat on the Sea of Life, crying out in fear and sorrow.

Tears filled Brae's eyes. He said to the Messenger, "Please send me to help them."

Looking out over the white-capped water, Brae saw the floating debris of a broken ship. Then he saw a man in the water. He threw out a lifeline and drew him in to safety.

The stranger stood shivering before Brae, rivulets of icy water drizzling from his short-cropped gray hair, trickling down his face and glistening like tiny diamonds on his salt-and-pepper beard.

He grasped Brae's hand. "Thank you," he gasped. "Thank you... for... saving my life."

With that, the poor man collapsed onto the deck. Brae half carried, half dragged the drenched man below deck. He put him in one of the bunks and piled blankets on the man, and then brought him a bowl of hot soup.

"When you have rested," Brae said, "I would like to hear your story."

Back on deck, Brae stood long at the rail, listening for the sound of voices rising from the sea. A cacophony of voices filled the night—birds calling to their mates, lions commanding their prides, and wolves howling at the moon. But these were harmonious voices, not the voices of people lost in the Sea of Life. The voices of the lost were silent. Brae retired to his bed. Perhaps tomorrow they would speak again, and he would sail forward to find them, bring them aboard the ship, and invite them to join him on the journey to the Other Kingdom.

Brae rose with the sun. Following his nose to the galley, he found that the Messenger had prepared breakfast. The stranger looked up with a smile. Over a steaming bowl of oatmeal and dried fruit, he told his story.

"My name," he began, "is Mikhail. I was sailing peacefully on the Sea of Life when I heard cries for help. The wind drew me into the rushing channel. Once there, I could not get out again. I was powerless against the wind and water. My ship, *Good Works*, stuck fast on a rock and was smashed into pieces. I survived by clinging to the rock until you arrived."

"Where were you bound when you were distracted by the voices?" Brae asked.

"I seek the Other Kingdom," Mikhail answered, drawing a deep breath. "I was born in the City of Self-reliance. I had a happy childhood there. But one day, someone I loved very much became ill, and there was nothing I could do to help her. When she died, I left the City of Self-reliance and began seeking for something greater than myself. I discovered that in a place called the Cape of Conviction. Since that day,

I have followed the Great King Immon who took my place on the Hill of Death."

"I have been there," Brae said solemnly. With these four words a lasting friendship was forged, born of a common experience and a shared vision, a common quest for the Other Kingdom.

After a long silence made comfortable by their bond, Brae asked, "Have you met the Messenger?"

Mikhail nodded. "It was he who stayed with me in the churning currents of the channel, holding my head above water until you arrived."

"I sail with the Messenger," Brae said. "We would be honored if you would join us in our journey."

Mikhail nodded, too moved to speak.

Chapter Twenty-four:

Mikhail

Mikhail pushed away from the table and climbed the narrow stairs. He stood on the sun-bleached deck, tears misting his eyes. When his ship hit the rock, Mikhail had believed his journey to be over, his quest a failure, because his beautiful ship *Good Works* had been destroyed, its rich wood splintered, its canvas sails torn. Obviously, *Good Works* could never take him to the Other Kingdom.

He had wanted to give up, to sink beneath the swirling water, and let the current drag him along the rocks until his body was as broken as his ship. But he had not given up because he was not alone in the water; because somewhere deep inside him a flame still burned—a flame ignited long ago beneath the spreading branches of the silver birch tree.

Mikhail leaned against the rail, remembering. Anastasia had just died. He had wanted to die with her. Life had no meaning, no purpose without her. She was the light of his life—his anchor, his beacon. She was everything to him.

They had grown up together in the City of Self-reliance, married young, and started a career together as merchants. They had traveled the world together, built a lucrative business, visited exotic places, and met people of wealth and stature. And they had not forgotten the poor. Mikhail and Anastasia were well known for their contributions to the needy.

Then Anastasia became ill. Mikhail brought her the best doctors and the latest medicines. Still, a hacking cough racked her body, draining her strength and taking her breath away. Day by day, she grew weaker, more fragile. Helplessly, Mikhail watched his beloved fade away.

The day after her lifeless body was committed to the earth, Mikhail got on his ship and headed out to sea. He did not know where he was going. He did not care. Life in the City of Self-reliance had ended for Mikhail. He would never go back.

That is how he came to disembark at the Cape of Conviction, his life in ruins, his fortune meaningless, his heart ripped apart.

What had drawn him to the dreary shores of the Cape of Conviction? Mikhail knew that it was the grayness of the place—the melancholic whine of the wind through the tall white stones rising against the gray sky. They meant something! And he was desperate to discover anything of significance to restore meaning to his empty life.

He had stumbled ashore at the Cape of Conviction, believing

the city deserted. He was taken by surprise when the vigilantes who swarmed from the "Department of Justice" building arrested him. He didn't resist, but walked meekly into the courtroom, where he would be tried for crimes he didn't understand.

The judge, a stern man seated in a high-backed chair behind a polished mahogany bench, wore a flowing black robe. From beneath bushy brows, he looked at Mikhail in somber disapproval.

"Do you know the crimes that have been recorded against you?" he asked, looking over his narrow spectacles, frowning.

"No," Mikhail answered. "I have been a good man, a faithful husband, and an honorable citizen, dwelling most of my life in the City of Self-reliance. I have given much of my wealth to help the poor and have broken no laws. I do not understand why I have been arrested."

The judge nodded, then motioned to the bailiff who stood at his right hand. "Andrae," he commanded, "start the scene."

Rising from the floor, a mist covered one wall, and an image began to appear in the mist. It was a desert town that Mikhail recognized from long ago. A man was standing before a hostile crowd. He was calm, basking in a serenity that seemed out of place, as a mob of men shook their fists in his face, writhing like snakes in their rage. They bound him, beat him, and left him for dead, and still that sense of tranquillity covered him like a garment.

Mikhail saw himself standing in the crowd, looking on with disinterest. "How could I stand there doing nothing?" He wanted to look away, but the scene was not over.

He saw someone from the mob approach him. He knew this man.

He was a merchant. Mikhail didn't like him. He knew that he traded in humanity, selling men, women, and children into slavery. Yet, Mikhail traded with him, buying his silk and spices, his carved figurines and ivory trinkets.

The scene shifted, and Mikhail felt his face flush with shame, for there he was, eating at this man's table, ignoring his bloody hands. Mikhail trembled as he watched himself take out his bag and pass gold coins into the merchant's bloody hands. He could watch no more.

Mikhail pled guilty to all the charges filed against him. He expected no less than death for his crimes. He welcomed it. Death would come for him and end his useless existence, quiet the dull ache that throbbed in his broken heart. He could ask no more.

The judge rose from behind the bench. Lifting his robe with age-spotted hands to avoid the red dust that puffed around his feet with each labored step, he escorted Mikhail from the courtroom. He led him along a winding path that led up a gentle incline to the cemetery he had seen from the ship. On the peak of the hill, shrouded in the gray mist of morning, stood an enormous silver birch tree. Its branches soared above the mist that draped like a sodden blanket over the Hill of Death to embrace the silver-lined clouds beyond. Crickets chirped, and birds sang their melancholy songs, as the judge retreated down the hill, leaving Mikhail alone in the shadow of the silver birch tree.

As he sat there, his back against the trunk of the ancient tree, Mikhail soon became aware that he was not alone. Someone sat beside him, resting with him against the tree. Mikhail was not startled. It was as if this One had been there all along.

Mikhail closed his eyes. He was so tired. He did not sleep, but he rested—perfectly at peace in the presence of one he did not know—on the Hill of Death. After a while—minutes, hours, Mikhail did not know, for time had ceased to exist for him, sitting there beneath the branches of the silver birch tree among the tombs—he looked into the eyes of the one who sat beside him. It was as if he fell into them. He felt himself swimming in deep pools of mystery, and peace rushed through him like a river. He could not move, did not want to move. As the river rushed in, all the agony, the sorrow, and the despair flowed out of him.

Broken and mended, Mikhail tried to rise. Weak and wiser, he fell to his knees. His head bowed, he waited. The One beside him stood and placed a hand upon Mikhail's head. Strength flowed through him; power such as he had never known coursed through his body. "He restores my soul." Where had those words come from? They were unspoken, yet they echoed in the depths of his being: "He restores my soul."

Mikhail stood to his feet. He was alone. And yet he knew, somehow, that he would never be alone again.

He returned to his ship, *Good Works*, and resumed his journey. It was then that he crashed upon the rocks.

As he stood at the rail, Mikhail knew that he didn't need the broken ship; he needed only the One who stood beside him, as he continued his journey on the Sea of Life.

Chapter Twenty-five:

The City of Broken Dreams

The sun bore down upon the Sea of Life, and a gentle breeze billowed in the sails of the *Seeking.* Above the song of the wind whistling through the rigging, voices could once again be heard. "Help me," they wailed. But this time the voices came not from the sea but the land. On the shore ahead, the lights of a city could be seen, set upon a hill. As they drew near the city, the voices grew louder.

"We must stop here!" Brae dropped the anchor. When Brae and Mikhail went ashore, the voices ceased. Everyone in the city seemed to be in a hurry. Everyone was too busy to pay any attention to the two strangers who had come among them, everyone except one man. He sat on a bench in a crowded park while children laughed and played around him. His clothing was tattered, his beard unkempt. He looked as if he had not slept in a long time. He looked up through squinted eyes when Brae and Mikhail approached.

"What do you want?" The man asked, slouching deeper into his oversized coat.

"What do *you* want is the question," Mikhail answered, smiling.

"Nobody cares what I want," The man scoffed, his hands fumbling in his pockets. "Why should they? I am nobody!"

"Do you have a name?"

"I am called Odair, but I am still nobody."

"You don't have to be." Brae was in his face now. "Come, join Mikhail and me in our quest for the Other Kingdom."

"I don't know of any... Other Kingdom." Odair lifted his hand as if to brush away an obnoxious insect, then looked away.

"But do you not dream of a place where men walk together in harmony?" Brae asked. "Of a life that is mingled with the lives of others, with no man walking alone?" Getting excited, Brae grabbed Odair's shoulders and turned him back to face him. "Don't you want to fight the good fight, slay dragons in the name of the Great King Immon? Don't you want your life to mean something before it is over and you stand empty-handed before the Great King with nothing to offer in return for the breath that he gave you these many years?"

Odair leapt to his feet. "Stop!" he shouted, alarming the children who played nearby and sending them scooting off to another corner of the park. "In my youth I dreamed of that which you speak about but it is too late for me! I have lived a lifetime in this city of empty promises and broken dreams. I wasted my youth and am ready to end this useless existence."

He pulled his hand from his pocket. In it was a small packet. "This is the day I die! I have no spirit left in my breast to compel me to this quest. I am a wasted man." With these words, Odair opened the packet and poured its contents into a cup of water sitting beside him on the bench.

As he raised the cup to his lips, with a swift motion Brae knocked it from his hand. Brae and Mikhail knelt before the despairing man. "You must believe in that which you cannot see," Brae urged gently. "There is a kingdom far greater than the Kingdom of Adawm. If you could only know the price that was paid so that you could enter there, you would go with us and claim your inheritance."

Hope, like the tiny flame of a single candle, ignited in the heart of the despairing man. He stood uncertainly to his feet.

"Do something!" Dagog screamed to no one in particular. We are losing another one!"

Lucacius sat on his haunches. He knew what was coming, and he wanted no part of it. He was not going to risk incurring the wrath of Immon by interfering with the drama unfolding in the City of Broken Dreams. Not today. He had seen this scene before, and he was not in the mood to challenge the servants of Immon.

"Go!" Dagog commanded. "Tear those two impostors apart! Go! Get 'em! Lucacius! What are you doing slinking away from me? I am your master! Do you hear me?"

Lucacius melted into the shadows and was gone, leaving Dagog fuming in impotent fury. Lucacius was evil, but he wasn't ignorant. He had managed to avoid destruction at the hands of Immon for many years by knowing when to hide and when to go in for the kill. This was a time to hide. It seemed Lucacius had been doing a lot of hiding lately. He didn't like it.

Immon sat on his throne beside the Imperial Emperor watching the scene unfold in the City of Broken Dreams. They laughed as Lucacius did his disappearing act and Dagog, like a rabid beast, chased after him. They laughed again, this time with joy, as Odair, standing unsteadily, reached out his hand to grasp Brae's arm and committed himself to the quest for the Other Kingdom.

Unseen by the eyes of flesh, a huge whelter, long and fat, lost its hold on the servant of Immon and fell, screeching in fury, to the ground.

The whelter were one of Dagog's favorite weapons in the battle for the soul of humankind. They were slimy, wraithlike creatures whose nature was to wrap themselves around the throats of unsuspecting victims and slowly suck their blood. They replaced the blood with vile green poison that worked slowly but surely to numb the senses and cause humankind to lose his focus. Without focus, he might wander throughout the Kingdom of Adawm for his entire life span, unaware that he missed out on the quest for the Other Kingdom and lost his inheritance—until he stood before the Immon with empty hands, realizing, too late, the loss of his treasure.

The sun was setting over the Sea of Life when the three travelers reached the ship. The Messenger stood at the rail, waiting. He reached out a hand and pulled Odair onto the deck.

In the days that followed, the *Seeking* sailed once more upon the Sea of Life. Having known the misery of those wandering in darkness, Odair wanted to stop at every port along the way and tell his story. Some who heard it joined the quest for the Other Kingdom. Some walked away in sadness, not willing to accept a gift so costly. Others drove the servants of Immon from their shores and clung to the darkness that consumed them.

Odair stood often at the rail of the ship, gazing across the waves, watching for the next port while Brae and Mikhail took turns at the wheel of the *Seeking*, rescuing those who were lost at sea and crying out for help.

Their work did not go unnoticed. The citizens of the Other Kingdom rejoiced as the servants of the Great King were multiplied in the Kingdom of Adawm. But there was no rejoicing among the followers of Dagog, Prince of the Darkness. Snarling with rage, they gnashed their teeth and plotted their revenge.

Chapter Twenty-six:

A Daring Rescue

The Sea of Life flowed along the shores of the Kingdom of Adawm, where many people were born and died without ever really living at all. Not knowing the route to the Other Kingdom, Brae and Mikhail followed the Messenger's directions, now sailing on boldly, at other times appearing to backtrack the way they had come. Brae was not entirely surprised, therefore, when one day a familiar landscape appeared on the horizon—the Land of Lasciviousness.

At sunset, Brae and Mikhail went ashore, leaving Odair on board to guard the *Seeking*.

Brae stood once more before the huge bonfire, watching the naked dancers leap in and out among the flames. He thought of how he had failed when he had last stood before this fire in the Land of Lasciviousness. He shook his head. How many seasons had passed since that day? The boy who had danced before the fire had long since yielded to the maturity of years spent in the company of the Messenger. The boy had come to the Land of Lasciviousness in ignorance, seeking excitement. The man came in obedience, seeking to set other captives free.

Seeing Brae and Mikhail, the dancers urged, "Come and dance with us. We pay homage to the god of the night. He will be displeased if you do not join us."

"We pay homage to the great King Immon," Brae answered.

"Who is this King Immon?" A young man asked.

"He is King of Kings and rightful ruler over all the kingdoms of the world." Brae answered.

"He is no king here," a young woman said. "We have no king but serve the Prince of the Darkness, one whose benefits we all enjoy."

"All true goodness comes from the hand of the King whom you reject," Mikhail said. "Dagog, whom you call Prince of the Darkness, claims a false honor. It is not Dagog that sends the rain upon your fields and gives fertility to your livestock. It is the great King Immon who loves you and requires your allegiance—if you would not see death in this land."

"What do you mean?" the young woman asked, startled by Mikhail's allusion to death. "Would the king of whom you speak war against us?"

"It is the Prince of the Darkness that has poisoned your wells and blinded your eyes," Brae said. "Life and peace can be found in none other than the great King Immon.

"I am weary of all this talk," the young woman said. "Pay homage to your king and to our prince as well."

"The Prince of the Darkness, whom you honor, is an enemy to our King," Mikhail answered. "We have no desire to honor him."

The woman spat on the ground. "Then be gone! If you will not dance before the god of the night, our prince will be angry because of you."

Suddenly, the Land of Lasciviousness was in an uproar. An old man picked up a club and leapt at Brae, swinging the weapon with surprising strength. Brae held up his hands, trying to deflect the blows. Mikhail was warding off blows as well, as other villagers picked up sticks and clubs and joined the fray. Children threw stones at them as they fled for their lives. They outran the angry crowd, jumped into their boat, and began rowing toward the *Seeking*.

"Wait! Please...!"

Several yards down the shore a young woman stood huddled with three small children.

"Take us with you," the woman called. "We will not live if you leave us here!"

Brae looked at Mikhail. Was this a trick? Already the angry dancers, brandishing clubs and stones, had noticed the young woman and had turned toward her. The children were silent, clinging to her, terror scrunching their small faces.

"Let's go back!" Brae shouted.

Angry voices roared into a holocaust of rage as the villagers began running toward the helpless mother and her children. Raising their clubs above their heads, they shrieked and howled like beasts of prey!

Desperately, the woman stepped into the water and waded toward the boat, carrying one child on her shoulders and one in each arm. Brae reached out and pulled the young woman and her children into the boat just as the first stone was thrown. The jagged rock glanced off her shoulder before thudding into the bottom of the boat. She did not cry out, but quickly pushed the children onto the floor and covered them with her body. Stones and heavy wooden sticks rained down upon the boat, bruising, bringing blood.

It seemed to Brae that the young men of the land, who were only a few feet behind the woman and her children, would surely overtake the small rowboat. Just as he was about to despair, a lion sprang out of the forest. An immense beast with muscles rippling beneath a blur of tawny fur and golden mane leapt into the angry mob, roaring, slashing, and biting. It seemed as if the whole land shook, and the trees bent low before a strong wind, like subjects bowing before a King. Stones thudded to the ground as villagers dropped them like burning coals and ran for their lives. The young men, seeing the fate of their companions, turned toward a distant shore where they emerged from the water moments later and made for their village.

Brae and Mikhail returned to the *Seeking*, shaken but full of joy. They were welcomed by the Messenger, who wrapped the young woman and her children in woolen blankets, and brought them cups of hot tea. When they were warm and comfortable, the Messenger sent them below to sleep.

They would need their rest, for in a few hours another battle would begin.

CHAPTER TWENTY-SEVEN:

An Old Friend

The woman stood at the rail of the *Seeking*, her slender form bent backwards like a willow before the wind. Her upturned face was bathed in the reflected glory of a thousand shining lights, sparkling in the night sky like tiny suns. She stood without moving, absorbing the wind, the sky, the sea, and the solitude. Wrapped in tranquillity as in a blanket, she breathed in the quiet. As in the calm before a storm, the sea seemed subdued.

The Messenger approached quietly, not wanting to startle her. "Salina." He reached out to touch her arm.

She turned to look into his face without surprise. Smiling, Salina took his hand.

"I know you," she said. "You came to my village when I was a child. Miarrow and Miammi sat around the fire with you when Sodomon was Chief. Though Sodomon rejected you, my parents believed in you and remained loyal to Immon."

Her eyes misted over as she took a brown leather journal from a bag slung over her shoulder. Its pages were torn and stained, its cover worn from much use.

"Miarrow made this journal for me, and Miammi sewed the pages into the binding. They said I should write down an accounting of the suffering in the Land of Lasciviousness so that I would never forget the example of those who chose to suffer for Immon rather than remain in bondage to the Prince of the Darkness. I have written an accounting of all that happened after you left."

She handed the journal to the Messenger, and he took it, holding it in both hands as he carefully turned the thin pages.

"Sometime," she said, "I will let you read it. For now please tell me, are my children safe aboard this ship?"

"They are under the protection the Great King Immon, Salina," The Messenger said, placing the worn journal in Salina's hand. "Go to bed now. Sleep. You will need your rest tomorrow."

As Salina gazed into the eyes of the Messenger, peace settled on her shoulders like a garment. She returned to her children in the sleeping quarters below deck, a tiny bunk tucked into a corner of the galley. She pulled a blanket over herself and her three little ones and soon fell asleep.

Salina arose with the sun and slipped up the narrow steps to find the Messenger standing at the rail, gazing with a fixed stare at something far away. Following his gaze, Salina studied the horizon. The good ship Seeking was drifting with the wind toward a shallow bay lined with powdery white sand. Just beyond the narrow beach, mighty trees swayed in the morning breeze. Birds of paradise darted among the leaves, making their presence known with shrill calls.

The Messenger turned to Salina. "Do you see the dragon ship?"

Salina looked quickly over her shoulder. Far out to sea, on the edge of the horizon, was a dark smudge of cloud. She nodded.

"There will be war. Tonight. We must get you and the children off the ship. I have prepared a place for you among the Newah people. They are a gentle people and kind, but they do not know the way to the Other Kingdom. Go to them. They will treat you well, and in return you will open their eyes to the Kingdom. Do you see the smoke that rises on yonder mountain? It is the morning fires of the Newah village. You must go now."

Salina's children crowded around her, grabbing her hand, clutching her dress. She pointed to the boat that waited, bobbing gently on the swells.

"Get into the boat," she said. She helped each child over the rail and into the rowboat. "We are going up that mountain." She pointed to a white-capped peak that rose out of the morning mist. Seeing the bag of food in the bottom of the boat, she smiled. "We are going to find the Newah village, and they are going to love you—just as I do!" The children snuggled close to Salina as she settled in beside them and The

Messenger took the oars.

The Messenger rowed the boat the short distance to shore and helped the children make their way onto dry land. Salina accepted the hand the Messenger extended to her and stepped lightly out of the boat. He handed her the bag of food. When she turned to say goodbye, the Messenger wrapped her in his strong arms and held her for a moment, infusing her with his strength, his courage, and his love. Then, releasing her, he stepped into the boat.

Salina sang as she led her children into the forest. Even as she watched him row across the bay toward the ship, she had a sense that the Messenger was still as close as the air she breathed. She would only have to call his name, and he would be there. She knew that she would never, ever, be alone again.

The Messenger pulled hard at the oars as he returned to the good ship *Seeking*, thinking of the surprise that awaited Salina in the Newah village. *You will soon see, little one,* The Messenger thought, remembering an entry he saw as he turned the pages of Salina's journal, *that happiness is a possibility at times, even for those who do not possess the innocence of children.*

Peering into the waning mists of the morning, the Messenger saw that the rescue of Salina had not gone unnoticed. Sulfuric fumes boiled out of the dragon ship, polluting the earth, sea, and sky with the stench of death. No wonder the flag of the dreadful vessel was a skull and crossbones. Low-pitched chanting like a ritual of death rose, interrupted by the occasional shriek of an agonized soul above the taunting voice of Dagog, and floated over the water. It was the sound of terror, of pain, of evil. The Messenger longed to clap his hands over his ears to shut out the repugnant noise, but he held steady at the oars, for he knew that the battle was at hand.

As the Messenger climbed over the rail of the ship, he saw the little group of warriors gathered on the deck. They were aware of the threat that rode the seas, but he knew they would not have called themselves warriors. They had no knowledge of the power that rested upon them.

The evening passed, and the dragon ship launched no attack. The weary warriors huddled on deck, waiting. Fatigue, excitement, and apprehension eroded their strength, and they slept. Long after midnight, dark forms began to move about the dragon ship. The *Avenger* raised anchor and began converging on the *Seeking*. Under the cover of darkness, the forces of Dagog came, burning in their quest for blood.

CHAPTER TWENTY-EIGHT:

The Shadow of Death

The Messenger nudged Brae. "Wake up!" he shouted. "The enemy is upon you!"

In a rush they came, forms without substance, darting like bats through the deepening darkness, slithering like serpents over the rail.

Never had the good ship *Seeking* hosted such fearsome and grotesque creatures, for Dagog coveted this prize, this trophy of Immon. His call for reinforcements had sounded long ago, and creatures that served the Prince of the Darkness had rendezvoused aboard the dragon ship, waiting for this hour.

First to respond to the urgent call was Lucacius, an ancient wolven whose fanged teeth had devoured the flesh of many a traveler. The most powerful of his kind, he commanded a legion of wolvens, each of them as bloodthirsty as he was.

The Messenger recognized Lucacius. He remembered the dark ceremony in the shadowed wood of the valley where Lucacius was commissioned for the post of general over Dagog's forces.

"You have to catch them before they discover the tree," Dagog had instructed Lucacius "for it is very difficult to trip them up afterwards."

"How do they discover it?" Lucacius had asked.

"The silver birch tree is musical, though most do not know it," Dagog said. "The symphony played upon its branches sings always throughout the Kingdom of Adawm. If any subject of the kingdom hesitates, even for a moment, in his quest to please himself, he may hear the music and fall into its embrace, never to be the same again."

"What should I do if one should discover the tree," Lucacius said, "and be offended by it?"

"That one," Dagog had said with a sly grin, "is ripe for the picking."

The bloodsuckers, such as the one that had attached itself to Odair, swarmed across the gleaming deck of the *Seeking*, leaving trails of slime in their wake.

Less numerous, but more deadly among them were the green-backed whelter. These were the fast-acting "rattler" species. Their bodies were forest green with yellow diamond shapes on their backs. Their bite was painful, their venom deadly. Within minutes of attaching themselves to a victim, they infused the bloodstream with enough of their poison to deteriorate the muscles of the heart and shut down the nervous system. The whelter that swarmed from the deck of the dragon ship were vicious, ruthless creatures.

There were also the wists, ancient inhabitants of the Kingdom of Adawm. Once creatures of flesh, they were now translucent, like milky shadows, floating stealthily over the surface of the earth or water. Reeking of death, intent on plunder, shrieking and howling, they leapt upon their prey, the stench of their foul breath like toxic fumes, sickening all who came near.

Lucacius and others of his kind, whelter, wists, and myriad other deformed, demented, and deranged creatures, wild with the lust for blood, now crowded aboard the *Seeking*. The servants of Immon found breathing difficult in the presence of such odorous creatures.

Brae was the first to raise his sword. He was not afraid. He knew the power of the weapon he held in his hand. He remembered the day it had been given to him.

He was barely seventeen, and his journey had just begun. He had just seen his first glimpse of the beast, Dagog, and longed to turn back to the City of Bondage. Had it not been for his fear that Meriquoi would kill him, he would have gone back.

It was then that The Messenger had commanded him to kneel on the deck of the *Seeking*. The Messenger had taken his own sword from the sheath that hung at his side and raised it high. Brae remembered the glint of the sun on the sharp blade and the ruby handle radiating streams of blood-red light as the Messenger held it there. He had touched Brae's shoulders, first the right and then the left, and handed the sword to Brae.

Brae had looked at the sword, not comprehending. Never had anyone given him a gift. And this was no ordinary sword. Brae could tell by the light that shone from within the honed steel blade.

"What do I do with this?" he had whispered.

"You will know what to do when the time comes." The Messenger had answered. Then he had smiled, and Brae had known that no matter what happened in the journey on the Sea of Life, all would be well in the end.

The time to use this sword had come! Brae knew no fear as he wielded the weapon given to him so long ago. Evil creatures leapt at him in the darkness and were swiftly felled by his sharp blade. Brae fought bravely as the dark clouds swirled overhead.

The night was long. The servants of Immon grew weary; yet, they resisted the onslaught of Dagog. They would not yield to the Prince of the Darkness.

Addar stood before his throne, consulting with two generals, his eyes fixed on the drama unfolding on the great stage of Life in the Kingdom of Adawm. He glanced at Immon, who, unseen, was secretly directing the battle. He smiled. His son was commanding the mighty warriors of the Other Kingdom with confidence and power. The throne room was bursting with messengers from the battlefield. The hoard of warriors in service to Dagog had grown throughout the night. Reinforcements streamed from the dragon ship. For every dark warrior that fell, another arrived to take his place.

A legion of shining ones stood at attention. Why did Addar delay intervention? Though some may have wondered, none questioned the Imperial Emperor, for ancient history had proven his wisdom.

Another room in the palace bustled with activity. It was the magnificent banqueting hall of the King. Mahogany tables stretched end to end as far as the eye could see. Crystal dishes were laden with food that tantalized the senses.

Though all of the food was grown and harvested in the Other Kingdom, there were vegetarian dishes that smelled like steak, fish, and chicken—they even looked like meat. Other plates held steaming vegetables saturated in butter. There were sweet breads and garlic breads, white breads and rye breads. Tall goblets of deep crimson juices alternated with clear, sparkling juices.

In the center of each table was an enormous vase of fresh flowers that emitted a heady fragrance. Music flowed from the petals of each flower, blending into a harmonious symphony of joy.

A banner flew high above the place of honor. It read "Welcome Home, Brae, servant of the Great King!" Everywhere there was a sense of excitement, of anticipation.

The Messenger appeared at the throne, his head bowed, listening intently.

Then Immon spoke. "It is time to bring our servant home," he said. He settled on his throne. Soon, his beloved servant would arrive. He could hardly wait to embrace him, to say to him before all the citizens of the Other Kingdom, "You have done well and proven yourself a good and faithful servant.

The Messenger nodded, then stepped back into the realm of the Kingdom of Adawm.

The Messenger stood beside Brae. He loved the celebration of homecoming, but he dreaded the process. There was always pain, always sorrow for those who were left behind.

Brae's sword flashed through the air, decapitating a long, sleek whelter that had launched itself at him from the mast. He whirled, catching one of Lucacius' kind under the chin just before its bared fangs buried themselves in his neck. Brae twisted back around, his sword reaching for the wist that had thrust a blood-encrusted dagger at his heart. Brae's sword found its mark, but not before the dagger ripped through his shirt, finding the soft flesh beneath, puncturing his left lung.

The Messenger flinched, feeling the pain in his own side as Brae was wounded. A crimson stain spread across Brae's chest. He looked surprised but did not fall. Holding one hand over his heart, he continued to fight with the other, though he felt his strength flowing out of him.

In the throne room, Immon rose to his feet. "It is enough!" he shouted, releasing a legion of shining warriors to enter the battle. Like northern lights, the warriors streaked through the night sky. Dark warriors fell like rain before the warriors of light.

A whelter had wrapped its wraithlike body around Mikhail's neck and was about to sink its fangs into the jugular vein. Within seconds, deadly poison would enter his bloodstream. Still he fought, not granting even so much as a glance to the slimy creature wrapped around his neck. A shining warrior flicked the whelter with the end of his sword, dumping him, shrieking and writhing, into the water, where vile green poison emptied out of him and dispersed into the depths of the sea.

From aboard the dragon ship, Dagog shouted, "Fire the cannon!"

As the dragon ship's cannon was fired, one of Immon's warriors reached out his hand and caught the fiery ball, flinging it back upon the dragon ship with great strength.

There was a tremendous explosion. The waters leapt high into the sky as if to douse the stars. The dragon ship splintered into a thousand pieces and disappeared. All grew calm. The great noise and light of the explosion subsided, and the rosy fingers of dawn spread across the horizon. In the transition, an immense dark shadow left the shattered dragon ship and returned to the region of the air that was his domain.

The servants of Immon were exhausted, but victorious. The Sea of Death was behind them. Before them, sparkling like diamonds in the morning sun was a ribbon of crystal.

"The Crystal River," murmured the Messenger.

Chapter Twenty-nine:

The Crossing

The Crystal River flowed along the edge of the Sea of Life bordering the Other Kingdom. Its shores were lined with golden avenues. Trees grew in profusion along the fertile banks, fragrant fruit dripping from their fingers. The travelers were so enchanted by the Crystal River and the land beyond it that no one noticed Brae, slumped on the deck of the *Seeking*. The Messenger knelt beside him.

"You are wounded," the Messenger said.

"It is... over." Brae coughed as he struggled to speak. Blood covered his shirt under the blanket wrapped tightly around him.

Hearing Brae cough, Mikhail rushed to his side. "Oh, Messenger, save him!" Mikhail pleaded.

The Messenger touched Brae's shoulder. Tears glistened in his eyes. "It is finished," he said.

Brae felt strength flow through him at the touch of the Messenger's hand. He stood to his feet. Suddenly, he felt as light as air. He stepped over the rail into the warm waters of the Crystal River. That is when he first glimpsed the land on the other side and recognized it as the Other Kingdom. "I made it!" He laughed and cried and tried to wade faster though the water to get to the other side.

A crowd stood at the water's edge, clapping and cheering, urging Brae on. A dark-skinned woman with long ebony hair, clothed in a white robe that shone like the noonday sun, raced through the crowd. Belita! Brae reached out for her.

At the river's edge, she paused. Music so beautiful and tender that it took Brae's breath away flowed from the flowers, the trees, and even the rocks. Belita danced beside the river—swaying with the gentle rhythm of the music, turning graceful pirouettes. She laughed and waved at Brae.

He waved back at her, moving faster toward the shore. Then he was swimming, fighting the current that threatened to pull him back to the boat, back to his journey. The crowd was yelling now, encouraging, "You can make it!"

The current grew stronger as Brae neared the other shore. Sharp jagged rocks jutted up from the riverbed, barely visible above the water's surface. One came out from the crowd and stretched out his hands. The folds of his robe fell back, and his scars could clearly be seen.

"You are The Wounded One," Brae gasped, as he came out of the water, his eyes fixed on the scars that crisscrossed the arms and hands that drew him onto the shores of the Other Kingdom.

Immon nodded, his face only inches from Brae's. His shoulder-length brown hair, parted in the middle, barely concealed the puncture wounds on his forehead. "I am the Wounded One who heals your wounds." He confirmed.

Brae looked down at the familiar scars that he had tried so hard to conceal on his own body: the scars from Meriquoi's whip, the scars from the beating in the Port of Plenty, the scars from the ropes that bound him in the Land of Lasciviousness.

Now, for the first time, Brae could see the abrasions on his heart, as if a light shone from within and illuminated him from the inside out. Brae watched in wonder as the jagged wounds and gaping holes in his heart mended. Sorrow and shame, rejection and fear, guilt and regret, all of these and other pains that Brae could not recognize drained out of him, and the holes closed up, the rends were repaired. Final healing, full and complete, was his as he stood in the presence of the Wounded One who healed all his wounds and freed him from all his pain. Immon took his arm and led him along the path to the banquet hall beside the throne room, where a feast was prepared and a banner proclaimed WELCOME HOME.

Then, as if a curtain had been drawn, the Crystal River was no more. The Other Kingdom could not be seen. The good ship *Seeking* bobbed gently on the Sea of Life.

Mikhail and Odair stood still, too amazed to speak. After a while, they turned to the Messenger.

His eyes were filled with tears. "Unfurl the sails," he said, "and lift the anchor. There are other victories to be won."

Chapter Thirty:

In Search of the Lost

The sun was setting over the Sea of Life as Mikhail turned the good ship *Seeking* into the wind. He grieved as the tall sails billowed, sweeping the ship out into the open sea. Cumulus clouds, like great gray pillows, spread across the horizon, weeping warm drops of rain. They pattered softly against the weathered deck, soaking the weary captain, who stood in silence at the helm, a battle raging in his heart.

He knew the will of Immon, but he wanted to be left alone with his grief. He wanted to cross the Crystal River into the Other Kingdom and walk the golden paths beneath the trees with Brae. He wanted to go home.

The Messenger laid a gentle hand on Mikhail's arm. "The lost still wait," he reminded.

Tears began to flow down the good man's face. Mikhail closed his eyes. He was tired. He wanted to go to bed, to sleep, to pretend that today had never happened. He would wake up, and Brae would be standing on the deck, at the wheel, guiding the *Seeking* on yet another journey.

When he opened his eyes, he gasped at the scene before him. The heavy gray clouds had parted in the center—like a blanket that has been split down the middle and furled back. Brilliant rays of sunshine streamed through the opening, bathing the ship in golden light. A rainbow burst through the clouds on each side of the stream of light, creating an archway through which the *Seeking* sailed. Its tall canvas sails glistened in the light like milky pearls against the emerald sea.

Mikhail understood that if he sailed through the rainbow-enshrouded archway and basked in the warm glow of cleansing light, then he could not—would not—turn back.

Suddenly, Mikhail knew—though he could not say how he knew—that those who cross over the great sea to attain the Other Kingdom are only a breath away from those who journey still on the Sea of Life.

So much thinking made Mikhail's head hurt, but his heart grew lighter with the hope ignited by such thoughts.

The Messenger laid a hand on Mikhail's arm. "There is a saying in the Book," he said, holding up a thick book that bore the name, *Ancient Book of Mysteries.* Mikhail knew of this book. Brae read it every day, near the end, and claimed that its pages were illuminated from within the book itself.

A sudden loneliness, so acute that it took Mikhail's breath away swept over the grieving man. But the memory that wrenched his heart was not of Brea but of the beautiful woman that he had loved since his youth. His empty arms ached to hold her. *How can the death of one provoke such longing for another?* Mikhail could almost smell the perfume Anastasia wore just for him, imported by their own ships from a land across the great sea. *If only she could sail with me now, on the* Seeking, *what an adventure that would be.*

But perhaps she does. Perhaps she is as close as the clouds that swathe the sails of the Seeking.

Mikhail rubbed his temple and shook his head, trying to clear his mind. *Where are all these thoughts coming from? They are too lofty for me. Yet, it is said that grief often tills the soil of the mind, making it more receptive to truths disdained before the suddenness of death.*

Mikhail's jaw set with new determination. He would sail into tomorrow with the Messenger at his side and dedicate his life to rescuing those caught in Dagog's deception.

"Immon, king of the kingdom that rules my heart and my allegiance, if you send me I will go and pay any price, suffer any loss to show the way to those who are willing to forsake the cities of their birth and enter upon the fair shores of the Other Kingdom."

But Mikhail was not to sail upon the seas. The Messenger pointed starboard to a desolate land. "There," he said, "is where you shall go."

Mikhail stared at the tops of the trees tossing against the hard blue sky, as seagulls wheeled above the branches, calling to each other.

He jumped as a scream pierced the sky and a shrill voice shrieked in response. The seagulls continued to circle, but they were silent now.

"You will not see me as you journey," the Messenger continued, "but I will be with you, as close as the air you breathe."

Sensing Mikhail's disappointment, the Messenger said, "Trust not in what you see, Mikhail, but in whom you know, and you will vanquish every foe that comes against you." Then the Messenger held out to him the *Ancient Book of Mysteries*. "Take this," he said.

"Who am I to possess the *Ancient Book?*" Mikhail drew back. "This book has been treasured by others far more worthy than I."

"Take it, Mikhail—" the Messenger placed it in his hands—"for you will have need of it."

Dropping anchor in a small bay, Mikhail and the Messenger lowered the skiff and rowed the short distance to shore. They stood at the intersection of sand and sea, looking into the vast shadowed darkness of a wild and perilous land.

About the Author

Born in Newport, Arkansas, Linda Settles spent the first years of her life in a three-room house across the road from a cotton patch. The family had all the necessary commodities, an outhouse, chickens, and a dilapidated Ford. Linda was the oldest daughter, and her brother, Eddie (eleven months older than she), was her best friend and protector. When Eddie died at age nine, Linda suddenly became the eldest in a family that grew until there were six children, an absentee mother, and a domineering father.

Linda has always loved writing. As a teenager she wrote poetry that was often published in *Latchstrings*, a newspaper in North Little Rock. Having noticed her poems, the head of Poet's Roundtable of Arkansas offered her an honorary position in the Roundtable with a view to mentoring her, and invited her to their annual banquet to be introduced. Linda's father refused to let her attend, but she didn't give up writing. She wrote a poem about real estate that the *Arkansas Democrat* newspaper used to launch its real estate section. Linda was photographed and written up in the first edition.

Linda grew up and fled the Ozarks for Michigan, where she discovered how wonderful life is when one is free to enjoy it. She soon met and married Michael Settles. Linda and Mike are excited about the direction their life has taken and are thrilled to write each new chapter in the book of their personal Journey on the Sea of Life. There is much to be done before they reach the Other Kingdom, and they look forward to doing it.

Also Available in this Series

Tried by Fire
THE SECOND BOOK OF JOURNEYS

Introduction to Tried by Fire

BY SALINA, FRIEND OF THE MESSENGER

Today the Messenger left us. I know he said he would be with us always, but I watched the Seeking raise her sails. I saw the glimmer of the sun upon the sea, split by the prow of the old ship, and the foaming swells that followed in her wake. I waved to the Messenger as he stood at the rail, waved goodbye to the one who sat beside me at our fires, and wrapped his arms around me as I slept.

The drums have not ceased to sound since the Messenger set sail. Miammi and Miarrow whisper as they look toward Sodomon's tent. I have been told to gather my things, for tomorrow the Resisters will move deeper into the jungle.

Sadie refuses to go with us. "My place is here," she says with her jaw set. Who will teach me the art of words, Sadie, if you do not go with us?

Sodomon stalks through the village, stabbing at the ground with his palero—the stout stick that he uses on the heads of wild dogs that charge out of the jungle, and on the back of any person unfortunate enough to get in his way.

I don't know if I am going to like our new way of life, but Surice, our new leader, says it is better to live in the jungle than to perish in the fire.

Into the Unknown

THE THIRD BOOK OF JOURNEYS

Mikhail, the merchant sailor whose ship crashed on the Sea of Life, journeys into the depths of a wild and desolate land. His faith will be tested by loneliness and his courage by warfare with invisible enemies who are committed to his destruction. This allegorical story of courage, determination, and unconditional love will draw readers into a deeper relationship with the three sovereigns who interact in the affairs of the kingdom of Adawm.

Edict House
Publishing Group, LLC

EDICT HOUSE PUBLISHING GROUP, LLC

Philosophy Statement

Remember the king's edict in the story of Esther? King Xerxes had signed a decree assuring the annihilation of the Jewish people. The decree could not be rescinded, though Xerxes regretted it, for he had sealed it with his royal signet ring. The Jews were saved by Mordecai's suggestion that they be allowed to arm themselves. Xerxes issued an edict granting the Jews in every city the rights to assemble and to protect themselves and their families.

We live in an era when the values that sustain the health of our nation and our lives are challenged on all sides. History records the age-old question "What is truth?" The answer requires a lifelong search. Every individual has the right and the responsibility to speak the truth as he or she perceives it, for absolute truth is our only defense against the destruction of our values and our lives.

We at Edict House Publishing Group, LLC are committed to publishing books that will facilitate the search for truth as they encourage, enlighten, and entertain our readers.